D1157226

FAIRY TALES

The

VILLain's

VERSION

FAIRY TALES

The VILLAIN'S VERSION

Kaye Umansky

Conkers

onkers

First published in 2019 in Great Britain by
Barrington Stoke Ltd
18 Walker Street, Edinburgh, EH3 7LP

www.barringtonstoke.co.uk

A CIP catalogue record for this book is available
from the British Library upon request

ISBN: 978-1-78112-853-4

Printed and bound by CPI Group (UK) Ltd, Croydon, CR0 4YY

For Hannah, Luke, Alice and Scarlett

CONTENTS

The Queen's TALE

The Stepsisters' STORY

The 13th FAIRY

The Wickedest WITCH in the World

Have Some WICKED FUN with the Villains ...

The Queen's TALE

ILLUSTRATED BY
Alexandre Honoré

The Magic Mirror

Look. How many times do I have to say this?

No one ever seems to get it, so I will repeat it yet again.

I never wanted the stupid mirror in the first place!

The mirror was a present from my new husband, King Frank. We hadn't been married very long, and he was still at the stage where he was happy to spend money on me. I really wanted shoes, but Frank didn't take the hint. Not even when I left the

catalogue open at the right page with a big cross next to the red high heels.

The mirror was gift-wrapped. I tore off the ribbons, ripped off the paper and held it up. I didn't like the size, or the shape, or the frame, or the chain. In fact, I didn't like anything about it. The glass reflected my unimpressed face.

"It's *magic*, darling," Frank explained. He was beaming. So pleased with himself for coming up with such a wonderful idea.

Huh.

"I sent away for it," he told me. "You look into it and say a little rhyme and it tells you how beautiful you are."

Now, I know I'm beautiful. I don't need to be told. And I know a thing or two about magic as well. I'm highly skilled in witchcraft, but of course Frank doesn't know that. I've got a Seeing Pool in my secret lair down in the castle dungeons. It's state of the art and it tells me everything I want to know. The lair is also where I keep my bottles of poison, my chest of disguises and some other stuff I'd rather Frank didn't know about.

So I don't need a Magic Mirror. Besides, they are so last year.

"What's the rhyme?" I asked. I couldn't care less, but it was clear that Frank was dying to see how it worked.

"It's written on a card tucked in the back of the frame," Frank said. "Go on, darling. Give it a go."

I tried not to yawn as I turned the mirror over and found the stupid card.

"Read it out, then," Frank pleaded. He was really excited.

"*Mirror, mirror, here I stand*," I read. "*Who is the fairest in the land?*"

The mirror did a swirly thing that made me feel a bit ill. Then a big green face appeared. It was some sort of ghastly Genie. He had horns on his head and a ring in his nose. I didn't take to him at all.

Frank was really impressed. His eyes boggled. It was his first taste of magic.

The Genie leered at me and said, "*You, O Queen, are the fairest in the land.*" Then with a pop he vanished, and my own unimpressed face swam back into view.

That was it. Pathetic. It didn't even rhyme. Also, the Genie had a silly voice that didn't go with his looks. Sort of high and squeaky. Annoying.

"Amazing, eh?" Frank cried. "What do you think? Do you like it, darling? It was very, *very* expensive. But only the best for you!"

"Thank you," I said. "It's a very – um – kind gift, Frank."

Just then, Snow White skipped into the room. She's my stepdaughter. Frank adores her, but I'm not keen.

"Good morning, Daddy Dearest," said Snow White. She threw herself into her father's lap and showered his beard with kisses. Then she turned to me. "Good morning, Stepmother," she said. "Isn't it a lovely day?"

"It is, my love," said Frank. "What do you plan to do this fine morning?"

"I shall pick some flowers," said Snow White. "And then I shall go and play with my friends, the forest animals. I do love them so. But first, I shall sing you a little song I made up about bunnies. It's got a dance that goes with it."

"Isn't she wonderful?" Frank asked me. "So sweet. So pretty. So talented. So—"

"Mm," I said. "Well, I must be off. I'm going to the shops." And I stormed from the room before I said something unwise. Behind me, Snow White skipped around, pointing her toes and singing some drippy song about bunny rabbits hopping in the sunshine.

"Don't forget your mirror, darling!" Frank called after me.

"Tell a servant to put it up in my bedroom," I snapped. If the truth be told, I would rather it went down the well.

I ordered up the golden coach and went out for the day. I bought two new coats, four pairs of shoes, six dresses, a ruby ring with earrings to match, and nine handbags. I went to Boots and topped up on lipstick, nail varnish and poison. I also treated myself to coffee and cake at the best hotel in town. The macaroons were to die for.

I enjoyed myself. It was good to get away from Snow White for the day. There is only so much of her that I can take.

My Evil Plan

"You never use that Magic Mirror I gave you, darling," Frank said, a week or so later. We were in the breakfast hall, drinking coffee.

"Yes, I do, darling," I said. "I used it a few days ago."

"And what did it say?" Frank asked.

"Nothing new. It's very limited."

"You mean you don't like it?" Frank sounded rather sad. I didn't want to upset him. In fact, I needed to keep him sweet. The bill for my massive shopping spree would arrive any day.

"Oh no, darling," I purred. "I love it. In fact, I'll go up and use it right now."

Outside the window, I saw Snow White run across the lawn in a cloud of song-birds and butterflies. She had a baby rabbit in her arms and a small deer trotted at her heels. She was coming for her morning hug-in with daddy. I was glad of an excuse to get out.

I went up to my room and marched over to the mirror on the wall. I gave a sigh and said the rubbishy little rhyme.

"*Mirror, mirror, here I stand. Who is the fairest in the land?*"

I tapped my foot and waited. There was the usual sick-making swirly effect, and the Genie appeared. He had a glint in his yellow eye that I didn't like. He smacked his lips and gave a titter.

He said, "*You, O Queen, are the fairest here, but Snow White is a thousand times more fair.*" And he vanished, with a smirk.

Now, that was a shock! I can tell you I wasn't expecting that. Oh, she's all right, I suppose, with her hair-as-black-as-ebony and lips-as-red-as-blood and silly little teeth-as-white-as-snow. But a thousand times fairer than me? I don't *think* so.

I'll admit I was upset. *More* than upset. Hopping mad, in fact. I brooded about it all day. At tea time, I didn't say a word. I just watched as Snow White chattered away, buttering dainty little pieces of bread and babbling on about the tame fox that's taken to following her around. She calls it Mr Bushybrush. Frank, as always, was enchanted.

"Mr Bushybrush?" he kept crying. "Mr Bushybrush? Ho, ho, ho! My word, what a lovely, funny name. Did you hear that, darling? Snow

The Queen's TALE

White's fox is called Mr Bushybrush. How does she come up with it? What a clever little poppet you are, my love."

I had to get up and leave. To my mind, Mr Bushybrush is a wet name to call a fox. If I had a pet fox, I would call it Killer.

To make matters worse, Snow White had a new dress on and was looking even prettier than usual.

"Don't you want more coffee, darling?" Frank called after me.

"NO!" I snapped, and went down into my lair to brood and mix poison. Mixing poison always calms me down.

That night, I didn't sleep a wink. I lay awake and plotted.

I had to come up with a plan to get rid of Snow White. I don't like competitors when it comes to looks. It takes a lot of effort and money to keep myself looking young and beautiful, and she doesn't even have to try.

Besides, the girl was obsessed with animals. The horrid creatures followed her everywhere. There were hairs on the throne cushions and stains on the carpets. You had to check before you sat down, in case of fleas, fur balls or hibernating hedgehogs.

Song-birds had made a nest in the candelabra above the dinner table. I found droppings in the sugar bowl. It was not healthy.

By the time morning came, I had a plan all worked out. I would send for the chief huntsman and command him to take her into the forest and dispose of her.

Harsh, I know. But I don't mess about.

The huntsman wasn't keen. He pointed out that disposing of little girls wasn't in his job spec. Besides, he would feel mean.

I said, "Get over it. Do as I say, or you won't have a job at all."

He said, "I don't know ... Little Snow White. Such a pretty little thing."

"Yes, well," I snapped. "You're welcome to your opinion. Oh, and this deal is between you and me. You'll have to keep your mouth shut about it. And do it tonight."

He said, "How much are you paying?"

I said, "How does a purse of gold sound?"

He said, "Sounds good."

I said, "I'll want proof, of course. That you've disposed of her."

He said, "What sort of proof?"

I said, "Her heart should do it. Take a paper bag. Bring it to me the second you return."

He said, "Do I get paid now?"

"No. Heart first, gold later."

He shook his head and walked off, muttering.

I don't know. You just can't get the staff.

CHAPTER THREE

Surprise

The next morning, I skipped breakfast. If all had gone well and the huntsman had carried out my orders, Snow White was a goner. I didn't want to deal with Frank's fuss and bother when she didn't appear for their morning cuddle.

I went straight to the huntsman's house on the edge of the palace grounds. I pushed open the door and walked in. He was sitting with his head in his hands, looking glum.

"Did you do it?" I asked.

He nodded.

I said, "Well? Where's the heart?"

He pointed at the dresser. There was a soggy-looking paper bag on the shelf. I reached for it.

"Not that one," said the huntsman. "That's my dinner for tonight. It's mince. What you want is in the drawer."

It *was* in the drawer. Yuck. I took one look and made up my mind I wouldn't take it back to the palace. I didn't want it to leak all over the rugs.

"Put it in the bin," I said. "And remember – not one word. Here's your reward."

I held out a fat purse. I'd been through Frank's trouser pockets for loose gold. There was rather a lot.

That cheered the huntsman up.

I rushed back to the palace and ran up the stairs

to my room. For once, I couldn't wait to use the Magic Mirror.

I said the rhyme. *"Mirror, mirror, here I stand. Who is the fairest in the land?"*

The glass wobbled and swirled and the Genie appeared. He looked pleased with himself, like he knew something I didn't.

He said,

"You, O Queen, are the fairest here,

But Snow White, who has gone to stay

With seven dwarfs, far, far away

Is a thousand times more fair."

He was about to vanish, but I stopped him just in time.

"Hold it right there!" I said.

He stopped and said, "What?"

I said, "Are you sure about that?"

He said, "Yes. That's the rhyme."

I said, "It doesn't rhyme. Poetry is not your thing. But that's not the point. What was that you said about dwarfs?"

"I'll say it again, if I must," said the Genie. "*You, O Queen, are the fair—*"

"Never mind," I said. "It'll be faster to find out myself. I've got a Seeing Pool down in the lair – I'll use that. Now, buzz off."

I rushed down to my lair and made straight for the Seeing Pool. A Seeing Pool is pretty much just a garden pond with extra magical features.

I stuck a finger in the water and said, "Show me Snow White! Hurry!" Then I waited for the ripples to settle.

When they did, I couldn't believe what I saw!

The Genie was right.

Snow White was far from dead. She was alive and kicking, and had indeed set up house in the forest with seven dwarfs! Their house was a small cottage with a crooked chimney, set in a leafy glade.

So the huntsman had lied to me! He must have taken pity on her and let her go. Goodness knows what was in his drawer. It had *looked* like a heart. He must have got it from the butcher, when he got the mince.

I was tempted to go straight back and shout at him, but I couldn't tear myself away from the pool. I watched Snow White blow kisses as the dwarfs set off for what turned out to be the local diamond mine. I watched them dig for a bit, but it was so incredibly boring that I switched back to Snow White.

I ordered the pool to show me inside the cottage. Snow White was making beds and sweeping the

floor. The usual collection of birds and animals were helping her. She looked perfectly happy and healthy. Arrgh! What a disaster!

I wondered how she had got on, all alone in the forest at night. Fine, I bet. After all, she had all her little forest friends to protect her. They had probably led her to the cottage.

It seemed that my work was far from done. What should I do now?

My eye fell on my chest of disguises.

I Visit the Cottage

A few hours later, I stood outside the dwarfs' cottage with a tray of pretty things. I was dressed up as a ragged old peddler woman, with a floppy hat and hoop earrings. I was confident that Snow White wouldn't recognise me.

"Pretty things for sale!" I cried in an old woman voice. "For sale! Pretty things!"

Snow White poked her head out of the window and said, "Good day, old woman. What have you got?"

"Nice things," I said. "Nice pretty things. Ribbons, all colours."

"I'll be right there," Snow White trilled.

A moment later, the door opened and out she came.

"Look at this," I said. "A lovely pink ribbon. Just your colour. Let me thread it in your dress, my dear. Turn round."

She turned her back to me and I threaded the ribbon. Then I pulled.

"It's a bit tight," said Snow White.

I pulled even harder.

"I can't breathe!" gasped Snow White. "I can't – ah—"

And she collapsed on the ground. I couldn't see any sign of breathing.

Result!

I didn't hang about. I climbed on my broomstick,

which I'd parked behind a bush, and flew back to the palace. I felt a lot more cheerful. Frank hadn't even noticed that I'd gone. He was out organising the staff, who were searching all over the grounds for Snow White. He looked almost frantic with worry.

I hid the broomstick in a hedge and sneaked past. No one saw me. I rushed up to the bedroom, changed back into my queen's robes and stood before the mirror. I said the rhyme and waited for the Genie.

Imagine my surprise and irritation when he repeated word for word the same stupid remarks that he had made that morning.

"How is that possible?" I snapped. "She *was* living with seven dwarfs, but I've just been there and done away with her!"

29

"Ah, but she wasn't dead," said the Genie. "She only fainted. The dwarfs came back and took off the ribbon and she's fine again. You did a rotten job. What's more, the dwarfs suspected it was you and made her promise not to open the door to strangers any more. So you won't catch her out again that easy."

I said, "Want a bet?" And I stormed off back down to my lair. I'm not used to not getting my own way. This time, Snow White really had it coming.

I mixed poisons until I felt better. Then I had another rummage through my chest of disguises. I was tempted by the gorilla suit but decided against it. Even an animal lover like Snow White would think twice before opening the door to a gorilla.

In the end, I went for the old woman disguise again but with a head scarf. I changed the make-up too. I gave myself rosy cheeks and padded myself out with a lot of woolly cardigans and shawls. I even had

a different tray, with different stuff. No ribbons this
time. Just a range of fans, some necklaces and
a few pairs of cheap gloves.

Oh – and a poisoned comb! It was large and green. I put it in pride of place on the tray.

I examined my reflection in the Seeing Pool. Excellent. My own mother wouldn't know me.

It was too late to go back that day. The dwarfs would be home. I would put all the stuff into a sack and take it up to my bedroom. Then I'd have an early night and set off at first light in the morning.

My Second Visit

"Different pretty things for sale!" I called from the doorstep. "For sale!"

There was a pause. Then Snow White looked out of the window.

"I'm not allowed to come out," she said.

"And why is that, my pretty?" I asked.

"Because yesterday, a wicked old woman tried to hurt me. My friends the dwarfs only just saved me in time. They think she was my stepmother in disguise."

"Really?" I said. "That's the worst thing I've ever heard. Why would anyone want to hurt a nice girl like you?"

"Anyway," said Snow White, "I'm not allowed to come out."

"I understand," I said. "You can't be too careful. But you can look, can't you?"

"Oh yes," she said. "I suppose there's no harm in looking."

"Do you see the fans?" I said. "And the lovely necklaces? And just look at this beautiful green comb. Just pop your head out the window, and I'll comb your hair for you."

The second the comb touched her head, she collapsed again.

34

Really. The girl has no sense at all.

I congratulated myself as I flew back to the castle. The gardeners were dragging the lake and checking all the outhouses. It seems that Frank was in a state of collapse. Not only was his darling Snow White missing, but the bill for my shopping spree had arrived.

As soon as I had changed, I spoke with the mirror again. This time, I was sure I would get the correct answer.

But no!

Believe it or not, those rotten dwarfs had come home, found her and pulled out the comb. They had given her a herbal remedy and another long lecture about not trusting anyone. The Genie was thrilled to tell me all the details. Foiled again!

I was getting fed up with this. Fed up of all the disguises and the comings and goings and having to put up with the Genie, who seemed to enjoy his role as bringer of bad news far too much.

I decided to try again a third time – and this time, I would pull out all the stops.

Yet again, I opened my trusty chest. This time, I went for a long, hooded cloak. Instead of a tray, I chose a basket. Instead of ribbons and combs and the like, I would appeal to her greed. I would take along a basket full of apples. I knew she liked those.

Now, this was the clever bit. I would poison one of the apples. Not all of it. Just one half. If I could trick her into eating it, my work would at last be done.

The next morning, there I was again outside the dwarfs' cottage.

"Apples!" I cried. "Fresh rosy apples!"

"Go away, please," came Snow White's voice from inside. "I'm not buying anything today!"

"But I've got apples," I called. "Fresh picked this morning. Come to the window, young miss, and I'll show you."

She came to the window, which was closed tight. She shook her head and waved at me to tell me to go away.

I said, "Open up, dearie, and I'll make you a present of one."

She said, "No. I'm not allowed to take anything."

"Why not?"

"Because someone might have done something bad to it. It might be poisoned."

"Rubbish!" I chuckled. "What a silly little thing you are. I'll cut it in half. See? I'll eat the green side and you can have the red half. Look, you can watch me do it."

I sliced the apple in half with a knife and took a huge bite of the green side.

"Yum, yum," I said. "Ooh. This is some apple, this is. So juicy."

Snow White watched me eat it. I could see she was tempted.

"You see?" I called. "Nothing wrong with it. It's harmless. Open the window just a crack, and I'll pass in your half."

Squeak went the window. *Crunch* went the apple as she bit into it.

Thunk! That was her hitting the deck. She wouldn't get up this time. That apple had enough poison in it to floor an elephant.

"Cheerio, Snow White," I crowed. "I don't think we'll meet again."

And off I flew, back to the palace, where I once again stood in front of the mirror.

This time, I got the result I wanted. The Genie nearly choked as he uttered the words I longed to hear.

"*You, O Queen, are the fairest in the land.*"

Music to my ears!

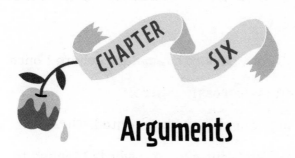

Arguments

I was looking forward to life without Snow White, but things didn't work out the way I planned. In the main, this was because of Frank.

He was obsessed with finding his missing daughter. He ordered posters to be put up all over the kingdom. He sent out town criers. He offered a huge reward for information.

He was so grumpy that I could never be bothered to talk to him. Not that he had anything interesting to say to me anyway. He was too busy whining about Snow White.

I came down to breakfast one day to find him weeping into his porridge. Again.

"Good day," I said. "Lovely morning."

"Oh, Snow White!" he moaned. "My little Snow White! Where is she?"

"I'm sorry, but I haven't a clue," I said. "Pass the marmalade."

"How I miss her!" he wailed. "How I long for a sight of her pretty face. What shall I do without her?"

"Finish your porridge, for a start," I said. "It's getting cold."

"How can I think of eating?" he sobbed. "She could be starving in a hedge somewhere."

"Indeed," I said. "Do you want that last piece of toast, or shall I have it?"

"I don't care about toast!" Frank roared. "And I do

think you could show a bit more pity for me."

"Oh, I do pity you, darling," I said. "It's just that I need a good breakfast because I'm off to the shops. I might be out all day."

"The shops?" snapped Frank. "Surely you're not going to the shops *again*? How many more clothes do you need? I've only just settled the bill for your last trip."

"I am the Queen," I reminded him. "I'm supposed to look nice. After all, I'm the fairest in the land. I like to dress the part."

"Perhaps," said Frank. He sounded rather cold. "Perhaps. But you're costing me a fortune. I shall be shelling out a great deal of money for the reward when my darling Snow White returns."

"If she returns," I said. It slipped out before I could stop myself.

"What are you saying?" asked Frank.

"Well, she ran away, didn't she?" I said. "That might mean she wasn't happy here. She might prefer to stay where she is happy." I helped myself to a muffin. "Mmm. These are rather nice."

"She didn't run away!" roared Frank. "Why would she run away from her daddy, who loves her? It's clear she has been kidnapped."

"Or eaten by bears," I said. Oops. That was the wrong thing to say.

"Bears!" Frank wailed. "Oh no! Bears! How could you even think such a terrible thing?"

"I'm just being practical," I said. "Do stop being such a baby, Frank. She's gone. Deal with it."

"Cruel!" he gasped. "You are a cruel woman with a cold heart! I sometimes wish I had never married you!"

He got up and stormed out of the room. I was left to finish the last of the muffins.

The Queen's TALE

I stayed out of his way over the next week. I ate my meals in my room. Out of spite, I went to the shops every day. If there's one thing I cannot stand, it is meanness. So I ordered myself a whole new wardrobe.

I chose new carpets to replace the ones Snow White's animals had destroyed.

I replaced my broomstick and treated myself to a fabulous set of designer suitcases that cost more than a small house.

I threw the mirror in the bin. I wouldn't be needing that again.

CHAPTER SEVEN

The Letter

A number of times, I tried to seek out the huntsman. I wanted to confront him about letting Snow White go and to take back the purse of gold. But any time I went to his house, he was never in.

I had just returned from yet another failed trip, when something happened that I didn't see coming. The postman was walking down the path with a jolly whistle. We didn't speak. I'm the Queen. I don't talk to postmen.

I was creeping past the breakfast hall, trying to avoid Frank, when I heard a sudden cry.

"She's alive!" Frank shouted. "Oh joy! My darling is alive!"

What was this? I turned back and threw open the door.

"What?" I said. "Did I hear you speak?"

His happy face changed when he saw me. He went white with fury. He had a letter in his hand. He held it out to me.

"Read this," he snarled. "Read it, you wicked woman!"

I took the letter. It was written on fancy paper. This is what it said.

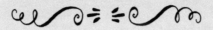

Dearest Daddy,

I hope you haven't been too worried. A lot has happened over the last two weeks. I hope you won't be upset at what I have to tell you.

Daddy darling, Stepmother has been trying to kill me. She asked the huntsman to do it, but he let me go. Then my dear animal friends led me to a sweet little house in the forest where seven kind dwarfs took me in.

Stepmother found out and tried to kill me three times. I was a little bit silly, but you know I always trust people. The first two times, the dwarfs saved me. The third time, she gave me a poisoned apple and they thought I was dead for sure. They put me in a glass coffin on top of a hill and sat by it day and night.

Then – would you believe it – a prince came riding by. He asked if he could take me back to his castle, and put me in a special room, with organ music and fancy candles. The dwarfs agreed, but when they lifted the coffin, the piece of apple in my mouth fell out. Lo and behold, I came to! Wasn't I lucky?

The prince is very nice. He is called Leopold. He is very handsome, with lovely curly hair. We have fallen in love and are going to be married. I am very happy and look forward to seeing you at the wedding.

Sorry to have caused such a fuss.

Lots of love,

Your little Snow White

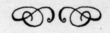

Oops.

"So!" roared Frank. "What do you have to say for yourself?"

Well, there wasn't much I *could* say, was there? It was a fair cop.

I threw the letter down and stormed from the room. Then I went upstairs to pack. It's a good thing I bought the designer suitcases.

There are plenty more kings in the world. Time to move on.

The
Stepsisters'
STORY

ILLUSTRATED BY
Mike Phillips

One Big Happy Family

Lardine

You know what makes me mad? I'll tell you. It's that everyone's on Cinderella's side. Just because she's pretty and ended up marrying Prince Florian, they all go "Ah! Bless!" and send her fan letters in the post. She gets other stuff as well. Posh dresses. Glass shoes. Flowers. Cake. Invitations to all the best balls.

My name's Lardine. I'm Cinderella's stepsister and my other sister's called Angula. I'm the soft, cuddly sister. Angula's all thin and sharp and bony. Just like a coat-stand.

No one ever sends me and Angula cake. What we get is lots of letters from people who don't like us – and they tell us so too. "Hate mail", the postman calls it. We don't get any invitations to balls. Not after what happened at the last one.

I said Cinderella's pretty. She is, in a boring sort of way. Long golden hair. Big blue eyes. Tiny silly little feet. That sort of thing. Angula and I hated her from the first moment we saw her. We'd have hated her even more if we'd known she had a Fairy Godmother. But we didn't know that, not then. And back then, she was just plain Ella. It was me that gave her her new name – the one that's stuck – Cinderella.

"Come, darlings," said Mummy, on the day we moved into Stepdaddy Hardup's house. "Here we all

are – a new happy family. I want you both to meet
your new stepsister, Ella. I'm sure you'll all be good
friends."

Angula and I looked at each other. We don't even like each other much, but we knew right now we needed to team up.

"Hello," said Cinderella with a shy smile. She put out her hand. We both looked at it as if she was passing us a dead fish. We did *not* shake hands with her and so she dropped it again.

Round One to us!

"Ella's bedroom is next to yours," said Mummy. "Won't that be nice?"

No. It wouldn't.

"I'm not sharing with Lardine," said Angula. "Her feet smell."

"So do yours," I snapped. Well, they do. Badly.

"Well, I don't snore," said Angula.

"Yes, you do," I said. She does. Very loudly.

"I'll scream if I don't get a room of my own," said Angula.

"And I'll sulk," I said. I would too. I really would.

"Don't worry," said Mummy. "We'll work something out."

Round Two!

At that moment, Stepdaddy Hardup came rushing into the room. He was grinning from ear to ear and rubbing his hands together. He still had a flower in his jacket from the wedding.

Angula and I were in our dresses from the wedding, our bridesmaid's frocks. My dress was too tight, and that put me in a bad mood. Angula's shoes were too small for her great big feet, so she wasn't happy.

"Ah!" said Stepdaddy Hardup. "The girls have met at last. What d'you think, eh, Ella? It'll be fun having two new sisters, won't it, poppet?"

"Yes," said Cinderella. "I'm sure it will, Daddy."

She didn't sound as if it would. I don't think she

liked the idea at all. Mummy said Cinderella didn't want her father to get married again. She didn't come to the wedding, anyway. She said she'd stay home and help get tea ready.

We think she was jealous because me and Angula were bridesmaids and she wasn't. Stepdaddy Hardup wanted her to be, but Mummy forgot to order her a dress.

"Good, good," Stepdaddy Hardup went babbling on, "Well, let's all go and have tea. Buttons has got a wedding feast ready for us in the front room."

Buttons is Stepdaddy Hardup's servant. I don't like him, and neither does Angula. He didn't help us off with our cloaks when we first came in. So we dropped them on the floor and shoved past him. We heard him tutting and muttering as he picked them up. Servants shouldn't tut. That's why I got a pair of scissors and snipped those stupid buttons off his jacket.

I have to admit the tea was nice. I ate seven sandwiches, three sausage rolls, five jam and cream scones, two helpings of trifle and a large hunk of wedding cake. Angula got stuck in as well. She may look like an ironing board, but she can stuff a lot of food in her mouth. Even so, I think I'm just that bit better than her.

Cinderella hardly ate a thing. She just sat there pushing a lettuce leaf around her plate. She didn't say a word.

"What's the matter, Ella? Aren't you hungry?" asked Mummy. She sounded cross.

"Not really," said Cinderella.

"You must eat, you know. Lardine and Angula have good manners. They always finish everything on their plates. Don't you, girls?"

"Yes, Mummy," we said, both at the same time, our mouths full of cake.

"I do hope you're not letting her be a picky eater, Fergus," Mummy said to Stepdaddy Hardup. She gave one of her frowns. "Growing girls need plenty to eat. Have a sandwich, Ella."

"No, thank you," said our new stepsister. A tear trickled down her cheek and plopped onto the plate.

"She's crying," said Angula, with a sneer. She reached across Cinderella and grabbed the last doughnut. I'd had my eye on that. I wanted it. I poked her with a fork.

"Oh dear," said Stepdaddy Hardup, looking upset. "Are you crying, Ella?"

"Just something in my eye, Daddy," said Cinderella. She patted her eyes with a napkin.

"I think you should leave the room," said Mummy. "We don't want a lot of fuss or drama at the table."

Cinderella stood up and ran out. Stepdaddy Hardup looked as if he was about to go after her, but then he saw Mummy look at him.

He didn't move.

"Spoiled," said Mummy. "Spoiled rotten. She needs to be taken in hand."

"Just give her time," said Stepdaddy Hardup. "She'll get used to it, I'm sure."

"Oh yes," said Mummy. "She'll get used to it all right. We'll make sure of that. Won't we, girls?"

"Oh *yes*, Mummy," we sang. Well, we would.

CHAPTER TWO

Teasing Cinderella

Angula

Well, Lardine's had her say in the last chapter, and now it's my turn. And just so you know, I *did* take that last doughnut, but Lardine took the last cream bun *and* finished up the trifle. And another thing – my feet may be big, but you should see her bottom.

On now to more important things.

We spent the next few weeks being mean to Cinderella. It was a lot of fun. We got her kicked out

of her bedroom, of course.
That was easy. Mummy told
Stepdaddy Hardup that it was
stupid, Cinderella having such a big
room. Cinderella pretended she didn't
mind. She said she'd sleep down in the kitchen,
by the fire, with the cat. She said she liked looking
into the glowing cinders in the fire. That's when we
started to call her Cinderella – after the cinders. I
came up with the name. Lardine says it was her, but
that's a lie.

Cinderella started helping Buttons with all the jobs in the house. She seemed to like it and even sang as she worked. We said "no way" to that. We told her she had a voice like a bull-frog. We said she wasn't to dance with the broom either, or make friends with little mice. Her soppy ways made us sick, we said. We took bets on who could make her cry first.

We cut holes in her dresses and told Stepdaddy Hardup it was moths. We threw away her shoes. We gave all her combs and ribbons away to a jumble sale.

In the end, she didn't eat at the table with us because Mummy said she was too picky and it was getting on everyone's nerves. Stepdaddy Hardup got a bit upset about this, but he couldn't do anything because he's so poor. Mummy's the one with the money.

Mummy was happy we were so mean. She said Cinderella needed to get real. She said children with no brothers or sisters got their own way too much and it was bad for them. Cinderella had to learn. Stepdaddy Hardup tried to argue, but Mummy said she'd stop his pocket money if he didn't shut up.

Cinderella pretended she was happy, but we often caught her snivelling to Buttons. Buttons hated us even more since we cut his buttons off. *We* didn't care. We hated him too. We kept dropping things on purpose, so he'd have to pick them up. We ordered him to make us snacks in the middle of the night.

We took the key to the kitchen cupboard and one day, when he was out, we muddled up all the jars. He keeps them all tidy. He couldn't say much, because he knew we could get him sacked.

We didn't want to get Buttons sacked. We were having so much fun being mean to him.

Mummy took Lardine and me shopping for new dresses. We didn't take Cinderella. I don't think she wanted to come anyway. Well, she'd have looked silly. She'd have had to walk into all the fancy shops in bare feet and rags. We left her cleaning the oven. We had a lovely day. We bought lots of gowns and jewels and ate cream cakes with cherries on the top.

On Cinderella's sixteenth birthday, we bought her an apron.

There was a bit of a fuss that day. Mummy saw Stepdaddy Hardup sneak along to the kitchen with a parcel.

"What's that you've got there, Fergus?" said Mummy when she saw him creep past the door.

"It's a present for Ella," said Stepdaddy Hardup. He went all pink and embarrassed.

"She's *had* her present," said Mummy.

"I know, dearest. But I thought her clothes were looking a little shabby. I got her a new gown."

"I see," said Mummy. "And whose money paid for it, may I ask?"

"Yours, dearest," said Stepdaddy Hardup in a small voice.

"I thought so," Mummy went on. "And what have I said about spoiling children?"

"But I thought, as Lardine and Angula have just had new dresses ..." Stepdaddy tried to answer back.

"That's different," Mummy said firmly. "Lardine and Angula have to look good when they go visiting. But Cinderella spends all her time in the kitchen or roaming in the forest. She'll ruin a nice dress. Give it to me, I'll take it back and get a refund."

"But ..."

"Give it to *me*, Fergus."

So Stepdaddy handed it over. Lardine and I smirked at each other. Things were going really well.

CHAPTER THREE

The Invitation

Lardine

That last chapter was rubbish. It wasn't Angula who came up with the name, it was me. And it was me who cut the buttons off as well. Angula does tell lies.

The invitations to the ball arrived on a Saturday morning. Angula and I were having a lie-in. Mummy had ordered Buttons to bring up our breakfasts on a tray. There are 95 steps between our rooms and the kitchen. You could hear Buttons puffing. It was great.

I stared at the tray. There was something else on it as well as my sausage, bacon, eggs, tomatoes, fried bread, mushrooms, beans, toast, jam, honey, pancakes, muffins, croissants, crumpets and tea. There was a big envelope with a gold border all round it.

"What's that?" I asked.

"Arrived in the post," said Buttons without looking at me.

"Give!" I ordered. I snapped my fingers. He handed it over.

I opened it up. How happy I was when I saw what was inside.

"An invitation! I'm invited to the prince's ball!" I shouted. "Hear that, Angula? I've got an invitation to the palace!"

"Me too!" yelled Angula. She'd come into my room and was waving an envelope about also.

I jumped out of bed, and the breakfast tray spilled all over the floor. We danced around the room.

When we heard that Cinderella was invited too, we weren't happy about that. Nor was Mummy.

"She can't go, Fergus," she told Stepdaddy Hardup. He was standing in the hall with Cinderella's envelope in his hand.

"Why not?" he said. "Lardine and Angula are going, aren't they?"

"Of course. That's different. Prince Florian is looking for a wife. Ella can't marry him. She doesn't know how to mix with posh people."

"But she's got an invitation," Stepdaddy said.

Mummy leaned across, took the envelope from his hand and ripped it in half.

"No, she hasn't," she said.

Angula and I smirked and headed for the kitchen.

Cinderella had her cloak on. About to go off on one of her boring walks, where she talks to little furry animals and helps poor old peasant women carry their bundles. We know, because we spy on her through a telescope sometimes.

"Guess what?" I said. "We're going to a ball at the palace and you're not. We're invited by Prince Florian."

"Well, I hope you enjoy yourselves," said Cinderella.

"Oh, we will," said Angula. "I intend to waltz with him all evening and make him fall in love with me while Lardine pigs out on cake."

"I don't *think* so," I said. "I think he'd sooner waltz with *me* than dance with someone who looks like a coat-stand and has feet like Cornish pasties."

"Oh yes?" Angula screeched, "He'd need super long arms to get round *your* waist."

That made me rather annoyed. But I let it go. We needed to pick on Cinderella, not each other.

"Where are you going, Cinderella?" I asked.

"Not to play net-*ball*," sang Angula. "Or foot-*ball*. Or volley-*ball*. No balls where you're going, that's for sure."

Both of us cracked up at this.

"I'm going into the forest to gather kindling," said Cinderella.

"My, what an exciting life you lead," I said.

"Why don't you just leave her alone," muttered Buttons. He was sitting on a bench polishing shoes.

"Mind your own business, servant!" snapped Angula. She dipped her fingers in the boot polish and wiped them in his hair.

We're really, *really* good at this sort of thing.

CHAPTER FOUR

Getting Ready

Angula

Lardine's only half right. *I'm* the one who's good at saying nasty things. I'm the queen of the cutting remark. Lardine's just a beginner.

Anyway. We both had a wonderful time getting ready for the ball. We went shopping again, and Mummy bought us two wonderful ball gowns.

Well, mine was wonderful. It was purple (my favourite colour) with orange ribbons. Lardine's was a nasty yellow mustard colour with acid green ribbons. They didn't have a big enough size for her, so she was bursting out of it, as always.

We got new shoes too, and new fans and handbags and tiaras. Mummy said she didn't care how much she spent as long as the prince fancied one of us. We had our hair done in a really expensive salon called "Hair We Are". I had mine swept up high on my head to show off my swan-like neck. Lardine went for blonde ringlets. The hairdresser left the dye on her hair too long, and it went a bit green. Lardine looked like a clump of seaweed had washed up on her head.

On the night of the ball, we made Cinderella come up and help us get ready. She pulled our laces tight (Lardine's had to be really tight). Then she put on our make-up for us and jammed our feet into our new high-heeled shoes. My shoes pinched a bit

because the shop didn't have size 11. But as Mummy

said, you have to suffer a bit to be beautiful.

Mummy and Stepdaddy Hardup were waiting

for us when we swept down the stairs. We looked

fantastic!

"Darlings!" said Mummy. "How lovely you look!

Don't they look fabulous, Fergus?" She gave him a

hard poke in the ribs.

"Yes, indeed," said Stepdaddy Hardup. "Lovely." But he wasn't even looking at us. He was staring up at Cinderella, who was leaning over the banister. She was all sad and dreamy.

"Well, come along, then," Mummy said. "The coach is waiting. We don't want to be late."

"Right," said Stepdaddy Hardup. "Yes, I suppose we must be off. Um – I'm sorry you're not coming, poppet."

"That's all right, Daddy," said Cinderella. "I'll have a nice evening in with Buttons, and an early night. I'll be fine."

And off we went. I was glad to leave that sad-o Cinderella behind.

We didn't know about the Fairy Godmother back then. If we'd known what was going to happen, we'd have locked Cinderella in the cellar and gagged her too, so she couldn't call out. But, sadly, we didn't.

All the way to the palace, Mummy kept going on and on about how we should be with royalty. She told Lardine not to eat too much. That's like telling a pig to go easy on the swill.

Then she said we had to agree with everything the prince said. She told us to curtsy low and laugh in tinkling high voices. We had to flutter our fans and elbow other girls out of the way. There was going to be a lot of competition, Mummy said, so we had to make sure we got in first.

The palace is on top of a hill. It has high towers and a lake in the gardens, with orange fish in. It was all lit up, and the courtyard was crammed with coaches. Footmen were running around helping the guests out of the carriages.

Lardine slipped when she got out of our coach and fell in a heap. Her dress split down the side. I thought it was really funny and I laughed and laughed, but Mummy was a bit cross. She said it didn't look good.

Then Mummy wasn't too pleased when I slapped a footman across the ear with my fan. Well, he

hadn't warned me to put my head down as I came out of the coach and I'd cracked it on the door.

It hurt. My head was sore and it was all the footman's fault. So why shouldn't he have a sore head too?

Mummy said the prince had soppy soft views about how to treat servants, and he might have seen me.

Anyway, I pushed my tiara over the bump on my head and Lardine held her bag over the rip in her dress. We were ready. Time for the ball!

CHAPTER FIVE

The Ball

Lardine

Just a few things before I start *my* chapter. Angula does not have a swan-like neck. She has a *stork*-like neck, which is something very different. And her dress was no way as nice as mine. But let's get on with the story.

Prince Florian *was* handsome, in a powdery sort of way. He was dressed from head to foot in powder blue. He had a white powder wig and a face with powder all over it. He stood next to the king and queen and greeted everyone on their way in. There was a long queue. I bulldozed my way to the front. Angula came looming along behind me and tried to trip me up. A few people tut-tutted at us, but *we* didn't care.

"Miss Lardine Hardup!" a footman called out.

"Good evening, Miss Lardup," said Prince Florian.

"It's *Hardup*," I said. "Get it right."

Mummy began to cough. A lot. You're not meant to correct royalty.

"I beg your pardon, Miss Hardup," the prince said.

"Oh, *do* call me Lardine," I answered, and I batted my eyelashes and made a curtsy. My dress ripped a bit more, but I don't think the prince noticed. Angula pushed me out of the way. She couldn't wait for her turn.

"Miss Angula Hardup," shouted the footman.

"Pleased to meet you," said Prince Florian.

"But not as pleased, happy and glad as I am to meet *you*, Prince Florian," said Angula. How smarmy was that! "I hope I can ask you for the first dance this evening?"

"Actually, *I* was about to say that," I chipped in, in a loud voice. I shoved Angula

out of the way. The prince didn't get a chance to reply. Just then another footman told everyone that the food was ready. We all rushed towards where it was set out, and we nearly got trampled.

Well, I have to say that we did our fair share of trampling too. The food looked very delicious, and we wanted first grabs.

The orchestra started to play and the dancing began. People began to whirl around the dance floor. Prince Florian didn't, because he was still stuck in the welcome line. He had to greet all the stuck-up show-offs who thought they were in with a chance.

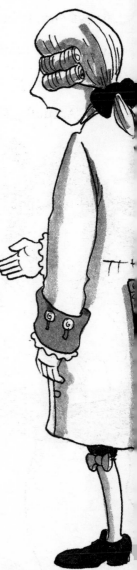

Mummy came up to me. She had left Stepdaddy Hardup over by a potted plant. He was nibbling on a cheese straw, looking sad.

"Now's your chance," she hissed behind her fan. "The prince is almost done. As soon as that last

89

girl goes, don't mess about. Get in there!"

We were going to do just that. Both Angula and I were ready to rush up and grab the prince's arms and drag him onto the dance floor. But we didn't. Something really odd happened next.

"Miss Terry Stranger," the footman called out.

Everyone looked round. The orchestra stopped playing. Standing there, in the doorway, was a dream of beauty. Well, if you like that sort of thing. I don't like all those dippy, girly colours.

The dream of beauty was dressed all in pale pink. Her gown had pearls

sewn all over it. There were more pearls in her curly golden hair. She held a velvet mask over the top part of her face. When she moved forward, you could see that she wore teensy little glass slippers on her feet.

The crowd murmured. Who was this beautiful stranger with the strange-sounding name? And why the mask?

"Show-off," snarled Angula. For once, I couldn't agree more.

Prince Florian didn't think that. His mouth had dropped open and his eyes stuck out.

There's no point in telling you much about the rest of the evening. Prince Florian danced with the stranger all night. Whenever there was a gap between dances, all the rest of the girls crowded around. Maybe he'd turn to look at them? He didn't.

Angula and I didn't bother. We decided to just eat a lot and give Miss Stranger mean looks whenever she waltzed by. There was no point in rushing up to Prince Florian and grabbing him. It was as if he was under a spell.

But Mummy wouldn't give up. She thought that Miss Stranger might leave early. If she did, we'd still be in with a chance of the last waltz. As it turned out, Mummy was right.

When midnight came, there was a bit of a fuss. Miss Terry Stranger came to a stop, right in the middle of a polka. She gave a little cry, backed away from the prince, turned round and ran off. She left one of her piddling little glass shoes lying on the floor behind her.

"Go on," Mummy said, and shoved us forward. "Grab him now! Go! Go!"

But Prince Florian wasn't in the mood for any more dancing. He fell to his knees, snatched up the shoe and held it to his chest. Then he burst into a long speech about coming around the next day and marrying the girl whose foot fitted the shoe. He added that it was a size 3.

That's when Angula had one of her tantrums. When it comes to feet, she's very touchy. Trying to get her great big foot into that shoe would be like ramming a prize cucumber into a tiny baby-food jar.

Angula gave a screech, hurled her fan onto the floor, jumped up and down on it and then kicked the food table. The table fell over with a huge crash, and all the food sprayed out over everyone. Then she threw herself down onto the floor and began to scream and bite the carpet.

There's only one thing to do when Angula gets like that. I sloshed a jug of lemonade over her head. She jumped up and hit me with a spoon. She was still screaming. I wasn't having that.

I whacked her round the ear with my handbag. My bag was nice and heavy because it was full of cake I'd put in it for later on.

Servants came running. There was a lot of fuss. The king and queen called Security.

Shortly after that, we left. Mummy was angry because Prince Florian hadn't noticed us. Well, he had, but not in a *good* sort of way. Stepdaddy Hardup was fed up because he'd had a horrible evening. Angula was in a bad mood because her feet hurt and

her hair was all sticky. I felt sick because I'd stuffed myself too much.

Then I *was* sick.

It wasn't a good ride home.

CHAPTER SIX

Back Home

Angula

For once, Lardine's chapter's right. When she threw up in my handbag, it was the last straw. In fact, I want to forget all about it and move on with the story.

When we got back, there was a large pumpkin by our front door. It was sitting at the bottom of the steps, which was odd. There were also some rats and some mice running around and making a lot of noise – squeaking and jumping. Did they know something we didn't?

A pumpkin? Cheeky mice? Rats with attitude? What was going on?

We found Cinderella in the kitchen. She was whispering something to Buttons. She looked flushed and was a bit out of breath. When she saw us, she and Buttons stopped whispering.

"Still up?" snapped Mummy. "I thought you were going to get an early night."

"I changed my mind," said Cinderella. "I had things to do." And she smiled an odd, secret smile.

She seemed cheerful. That was annoying. How dare she be happier than us?

"You're looking very pretty tonight, Ella," said Stepdaddy Hardup.

That annoyed us even more.

"Thank you, Daddy," Cinderella said, and smiled again. "Did you have a nice time at the ball?"

"All right, I suppose," said Stepdaddy Hardup. Then he saw Mummy look at him. "It was a very nice evening," he added quickly. "Most enjoyable. I think the girls had a good time, didn't you?"

"No," I snapped. "We didn't."

"What about Prince Florian?" asked Cinderella. "Do you think he enjoyed himself?"

"The less said about him the better," I growled. "He's got no taste, that one. No taste at all."

"Now then, Angula," said Mummy. "That's no way to talk about the man who might be your future husband."

"How do you make that out?" I snarled.

"Well, there's that shoe. Prince Florian's bringing it round tomorrow, remember? Both of you will get the chance to try it on. All is not lost."

"It's a size 3," Lardine said. "I'm size 9, and Angula's size 11."

"So? Sit with your feet in a bucket of iced water," Mummy said. "Try to shrink them a bit. And in the morning, we'll rub on lots of butter, so they'll slip in easier."

"What do you mean – the shoe?" Cinderella asked, all innocent.

"Prince Florian spent all night dancing with a Miss Terry Stranger," Stepdaddy Hardup told her. "No one knew who she was. She ran off in a hurry and she left a glass shoe behind. Prince Florian says he'll marry the one whose foot fits it."

"Really?" said Cinderella. She looked at Buttons. Something was going on, but I didn't know what.

"What's this all over the floor?" asked Mummy. She was bending down and pointing at the kitchen floor. We all looked down.

There was sparkly stuff everywhere.

"What can it be?" said Stepdaddy Hardup. He dabbed at it with his finger. "Snail trails, do you think?"

Of course, it was fairy dust, left behind by that stupid godmother, but we didn't know that then.

"Well, I don't care what it is, someone needs to clean it up," said Mummy. And she stomped off upstairs to bed.

Lardine and I hung about a bit. We wanted to make Cinderella cry like we always do. But for once, it didn't work. She went on smiling in her odd, secret way, and Buttons was smirking and giggling too. There was something going on, but we didn't know what.

In the end, we went to bed.

Have you ever tried sleeping with your feet in a bucket of iced water? Don't.

CHAPTER SEVEN

The Shoe

Lardine

The next morning, my feet were all blue and wrinkled. They looked like prunes. My toes were frozen together. I could hardly limp downstairs. Angula's were the same.

We sat in the kitchen, moaning like mad as Mummy rubbed best butter all over our toes.

"I can't feel a thing," I cried.

Well, I couldn't.

"Even if I get the shoe on, I won't be able to walk in it," said Angula.

"You won't need to walk," Mummy told her. "Once Prince Florian asks you to marry him, they'll carry you around in a litter until your feet are better."

"Do we really need to do this?" asked Stepdaddy Hardup. "It's not the end of the world if they don't marry into royalty, is it?"

Mummy sent him out of the room. She doesn't like him poking his nose in at such an important time.

It was lucky we didn't have to wait long for Prince Florian. Our house isn't that far from the palace, so we were one of the first he visited.

There came a knock on the door, and Buttons went to open it. In came Prince Florian, still handsome. Today he was dressed in riding gear. He looked even better without his wig on. With him was a servant who was carrying the shoe on a red cushion.

"Right," said Prince Florian. "Let's get this over and done with. Which of you ladies is first?"

"Me!" we both yelled. "Me! *Meeeee!*"

"Now, now, girls," Mummy said as she hid the butter behind her back. "I'm sorry they're so rude, Your Highness. It's just that they're both *so* keen."

"Tell you what, we'll toss a coin for it," said Prince Florian, and he took a penny out of his pocket. Angula chose heads and I chose tails. Heads won.

The servant took the shoe from the cushion and knelt by Angula's feet. Angula closed her eyes and crossed her fingers.

"Push, darling!" cried Mummy. "Never mind the pain! Push!"

As I thought, she couldn't even fit her toes in. The little glass shoe just dangled on the end of her big toe. It looked so stupid.

Angula gave a loud screech, kicked the glass shoe

off and had one of her tantrums. She fell to the floor and kicked her feet around.

Then it was my turn. My feet aren't as big as Angula's, but I take a double E fitting. All the ice cubes and butter in the world weren't going to do the trick. I knew that just by looking. No way was my foot going to fit.

I went into a sulk. Angula does tantrums, I do sulking. We each have our own way of doing things.

"Well, that was a waste of time," said Prince Florian. He was looking glad about that, which made me sulk even more. "Anyone else?"

"No!" we chanted.

"Yes," said a sweet little voice from the doorway. "Me. Can I try it on, please?"

"*You?*" I scoffed. "You weren't even there."

"Clear off, Cinderella, you're not wanted!" snapped Angula.

But the prince was staring at her in a funny way. His eyes were sticking out again. The servant ran up with the shoe.

It fitted. Wouldn't you know?

We all stood frozen. How could this be? Then Mummy passed out.

A fitting end to a horrible morning.

Fitting. Get it?

CHAPTER EIGHT

The Happy Ending

Cinderella

You haven't heard from me so far. Well, that's how it should be. After all, this is my stepsisters' story. But I thought I should have a quick word, just to tell you what happened next. I don't think Lardine or Angula will.

What happened next was, Florian and I got married, and there was gladness and joy all across the land. He's a very nice man, and we're truly happy.

My Fairy Godmother came to the wedding, of course, and so did Buttons. They both enjoyed telling my stepmother and sisters what happened the night of the ball. They told them about the pumpkin coach and the mice and the magic fairy-tale dress and ... well, you know the story. Buttons said their faces were a picture when they worked out that Miss Terry Stranger was little old me.

Daddy got a divorce. He seems a lot happier. He lives with us in the palace now. He and Buttons have got into fishing and spend a lot of time with the goldfish, down by the palace lake.

Florian was very upset when he heard how mean my stepfamily had been to me. He wouldn't let them stay in his kingdom. The last I heard, they were living in a rented bungalow next door to a fish-finger factory somewhere very cold. Siberia, I think.

I've written them some letters, but I never get a reply.

I suppose it serves them right – well, they were really horrid to me – but I'm not the sort to care. What's the point? I married the prince. I'm the one with the happy ending.

Post script

Lardine: Well, we told it in our own words.

Angula: We did.

Lardine: Do you think people will like us more now?

Angula: No. Do we care?

Lardine: No. Let's go and read our hate mail.

THE END

The 13th FAIRY

ILLUSTRATED BY
Stefano Tambellini

Hopping Mad!

Now, let's get one thing clear. I refuse to take the blame. You know what I'm talking about. That business with Sleeping Beauty. I have taken the blame for years, and it's time to set the record straight.

Now, I will admit that I went a bit far. You shouldn't mess about with curses when there are babies around. Curses can go wrong. I know that now. But I do have a bit of a temper. And I was very,

very cross at the time. More than cross. Hopping mad.

But you would have been upset too. Imagine your twelve best friends got invited to a posh party in a palace and you got left out. How would you feel? Insulted, that's how. Hurt.

Well, I say "twelve best friends", but they're not my best friends at all. The Twelve Good Fairies. That's what they call themselves. It's a sort of club. A club that I'm not in. Not that I care. I prefer my own company. I can eat when I want and sleep when I want. Wear the same socks all week. Leave the washing-up. Do what I like. You won't catch me being friends with that lot. I'm not friends with anyone at all really, but especially not them.

The Twelve Good Fairies wear ballet dresses and have silly flowery names. They meet in the woods every Saturday night when the moon is up. Then they skip around in their soppy fairy ring, dancing

on their tippy-toes and scaring the squirrels. When

they're all puffed out, they have dewberry tea and
fairy cakes, served on spotty toadstool tables by
frogs in bow ties.

That's when they talk about
me. I know, because one night I
hid behind a bush and listened.

I never get invited to their
parties. I wouldn't go anyway. I
don't like dancing, and pink doesn't suit me. I'm more
of a black rags person. I wear a pointy hat. I refuse to
have a flowery name. I prefer a broomstick to wings.
I'd rather be a witch than a fairy any day. Of course,
it wouldn't hurt them to ask me along, just to be
polite. But they don't. Just because I'm not like them.

They can keep their stupid old club. I don't care.

Anyway. I was really fed up when I found out that
the king and queen had a new baby and the fairies
were all invited to the christening! Nobody told me.

I only found out when I bumped into Fairy Bluebell at the Post Office. I needed stamps to send off the crossword. I do all the puzzles in the newspaper every day. I haven't won a prize yet, but you never know.

Bluebell never speaks to me, but that day she was bursting with the news and she couldn't resist showing off.

"Good morning, Grimbleshanks," she trilled. "Tra la la. What a lovely sunny day. I see you're wearing those horrid old black rags again. Don't you find them very hot?"

I could have zapped her there and then, but I didn't want to burn the other people in the Post Office. See how thoughtful I am?

Bluebell waved a big gold envelope under my nose. "I'm here to reply to my invitation! Isn't it too, too exciting?"

"No," I said. "Buying stamps is very, very dull."

"I'm talking about the christening," she said.

"What christening?" I asked.

"The christening at the palace," Bluebell said. "There's a new royal baby. Haven't you heard? Oh, of course you haven't. I forgot. You live all alone and have no friends at all."

"I don't live alone," I told her. "I live with Bill."

Bill is my crow. His full name is Big Bill Beaky. He's lived with me for years.

Perhaps I should tell you how I came to live with Bill.

One snowy morning I went out for some logs and there he was. A big crow, perched on a branch of my apple tree. He had merry little black eyes and a sharp beak. His raggedy feathers were fluffed up against the cold, but he had a cheerful air.

"Cold mornin', ma'am," he said. Very polite, very

respectful. And he had this wonderful voice. Not a harsh caw, like most crows. His voice was low, rich and sweet, like honey.

"It is indeed," I said. "Very cold."

"Yep," he said. "Winter's here, for sure. Worms is thin on the ground, I can tell you that."

I asked him in to warm himself by the fire. I made him some toast. We got talking. He told me he was a wandering crow who had travelled for many years in far-off lands and now he was looking to settle down. He said his wings weren't as young as they used to be. What he wanted now was a full belly and a warm fire, that's all.

He has lived with me ever since.

Bill eats bugs, in the main. He likes worms, eggs, frogs and mice for his dinner too. He's very easy-going about food, although he's not keen on slugs. He says they're over-rated. I always bake him a beetle cake on his birthday. He loves that. He always says, "Aw, shucks. You shouldn't have, Miz Grim." That's the way he talks – in a warm, slow drawl.

Bill doesn't say much, but when he does it's always interesting. Sometimes he sings in his deep, low voice. Most of his songs are about his travels. My favourite one goes like this:

I seen a lotta woe in
the time I been a crow,
but I'm livin' in a good
place now.

I could listen to Bill sing that all night. If he could play guitar, he'd be rich. But he's a crow, so he can't.

But that's enough about Bill. Back to the Post Office and Fairy Bluebell.

"Crows don't count," Bluebell said.

"Bill can count," I snapped. "He can count way past a hundred and add up and take away too, if you must know. And divide and multiply."

Crows are very clever birds. None of the fairies are as clever as Bill. They can't sing, either. Of course, as soon as I'd said how Bill could count, I realised that Bluebell had meant he didn't count *as a friend*. Which was not very nice.

But Bluebell didn't correct me. She wanted to talk about the christening.

"*We're* all going," she said. "We're getting new dresses and we're going to give the baby lovely magical presents, like Love and Joy and Peace. The christening is next Saturday at two o'clock. Are you sure you haven't got an invitation?"

"Must be my new postman," I lied. "He couldn't find the house, I expect. The invite must be delayed."

It wasn't, of course. It had never been sent in the first place. But I didn't want to let Bluebell gloat.

"You'll have to scrub up a bit if you do come," Bluebell said. "But I imagine they've decided not to ask you. It is a *palace*, you know. They have to think of the carpets. Your pointy hat and black rags won't fit in. And that awful, raggedy old bird of yours with his horrid sharp beak wouldn't be welcome. Not with a royal baby about. You'd both be a bit of a downer at a party. Oh, look, here's Primrose! Coo-*eee*! Primrose!"

Fairy Primrose fluttered over. She was clutching another large gold envelope in one hand and a card in the other.

The card was covered in glitter and little red hearts, and it said in dainty fairy writing:

Dear King and Queen,

I would love to come to the christening.
I will bring a very magical gift for your
new baby.

Love and kisses from
Fairy Primrose

Fairy Primrose and Fairy Bluebell fell into each other's arms.

"I'm posting my reply to the invitation!" Primrose cried. She was all pink and flustered.

"Me too!" Bluebell squealed. "Isn't it exciting? Everyone's going. Lilac, Rose, Violet, Snowdrop, Pansy, Daisy, Poppy, Daffodil, Holly and Marigold. Everyone except Grimbleshanks. She hasn't had an invitation."

They both stared at me with looks of pity. Well, pretend pity. In fact, they were pleased I wasn't coming. I gave a shrug, to show I didn't care.

"That's because there are only twelve gold plates," Primrose said. "Remember last year, Bluebell, when we went to the palace as guests of honour? When the king and queen got married? There were only twelve gold plates, I'm almost sure of it."

I was thunderstruck. Until now, I hadn't realised I hadn't been invited to the wedding either! Talk about adding insult to injury.

"Twelve gold plates and twelve fairies," Primrose said. "If you were there, there would be thirteen, you see, Grimbleshanks. You'd have to eat from the dog's bowl or something."

They both burst into charming fairy giggles.

"No problem – I'd eat off your gold plate," I said. My face was grim.

"I don't think so," said Primrose, and she tossed her curly hair.

"I don't think the plates are the problem," said Bluebell. She stared at me. "The problem is the rags and the pointy hat. And the crow. You don't fit in, Grimbleshanks. You don't have nice pretty clothes like us. You would lower the tone. Anyway, thirteen's an unlucky number."

"Ah, go and boil your head in an acorn," I said, and stomped off in a huff. I didn't bother to buy the stamps. I couldn't care less about the crossword any more. I just wanted to go and kick something.

I could hear them whispering and giggling about me all the way home.

I Stew for a Week

The whole thing played on my mind. I shouldn't have let it bother me, but it did. I stewed for a whole week. I lost sleep thinking about it. I wondered whether to write a stiff letter of protest to the palace. Then I remembered I didn't have a stamp.

The Good Fairies kept rubbing it in that I didn't have an invite. That didn't help. Little groups of them kept skipping past my gate, chattering about the stupid new frocks they were going to buy.

They made up a mean song. It went like this:

She's not invited to the party,

She's not invited to the party,

She's not invited to the party

And there's nothing she can do!

Then they'd all fall about laughing. And sing it again. I didn't find it at all funny.

I kept the curtains closed and pretended I couldn't hear. But of course I could.

I discussed the matter with Big Bill Beaky. He always gives me good advice.

"Bill," I said. "I can't stand this."

"Let it go, Miz Grim. Let it go," Bill said from his perch. "They'll get tired of teasin' you."

"I can't," I said. "I need to do something. It's really getting to me."

"Write a nice letter to the palace, then," Bill said. "Ask them to send you an invite."

"I haven't got a stamp," I huffed. "Anyway, it's too late to be nice now. I need to do something big and dramatic. I'm angry, Bill. I need to get it out of my system. Only then can I move on."

"Forget it, Miz Grim. Nothin' good ever comes of gettin' all riled up," Bill said.

"I'm not thinking 'Good'. I'm thinking 'Bad'."

"Ain't good for you," said Bill. "Thinkin' 'Bad'."

"I don't care," I said. "I'm thinking about a curse."

"A curse," said Bill. He gave a little whistle, put his head on one side and stared at me. "Hm. That's kinda strong, ain't it?"

He was right. But I didn't want to let it go. I'm good at curses. Curses are my style. I can curse louder than anyone I know, and I can magic up a nice bit of thunder and lightning to go with it.

"They won't forget a curse in a hurry," I said.

In my mind, I could see myself in the great hall at the palace. I would wave my wand about while everyone shivered in their socks. I would deliver a curse that would knock the spots off the Good Fairies' soppy gifts.

"Who you gonna curse?" Bill asked.

"Well ..." I said. "The baby, I suppose."

"Why the baby? What's the baby done?"

I couldn't answer that. The baby had done nothing.

"You sure 'bout this?" asked Bill. "I mean, I know you're angry an' all that. But ain't it a bit over the top to curse the baby?"

"It'll be fine," I said. "Don't worry, I'll plan it properly. I've got to make sure I get the words right. I won't *really* hurt the baby. I'll just shake them all up a bit. Show the Good Fairies some real magic. Teach the king and queen a lesson about good manners. Show them what happens when they upset me. Don't argue, Bill. I've made up my mind."

"OK, then." Bill shrugged his wings and sighed. "If that's the way you wanna play it."

"It is," I said.

"Just make sure you get them words right."

"I will. Ready for your worms now?"

"Yup," said Bill. "Bring 'em on."

He's always ready for his worms.

Pulling Out the Stops

So that's why I steamed into the palace like I did, on the day of the christening. I had it all worked out. I knew exactly the message I wanted to get across. I had learned the words of the curse off by heart. I had my wand. My temper was up. I was ready.

That morning, Bill had said he would come with me for moral support.

"You don't have to," I said. "I know you think this is a bad idea."

"Hey," said Bill. "I've still got your back. You an' me's buddies, right?"

Bill's good like that. Very loyal. I took him in out of the cold and he says he won't forget that. Even when I'm being unreasonable, which I am sometimes.

And so I screeched across the sky on my broomstick to the palace. Bill rode on my arm to save his wings. It's a fair old way and he's getting on a bit now. He says his travellin' days are over.

I flew down over the palace gardens. The broom's not as accurate as it once was, and I had to make an emergency stop.

I landed on my bottom in a rose bush, which put me in a vile mood. I was scratched and pricked all over by thorns.

"You OK, Miz Grim?" Bill asked as he zig-zagged down.

"I'm fine," I said as I picked the thorns out of my bum. I had a nasty scratch on my chin too.

"You sure?" Bill said. "Cos we can go on home and get you a cup of tea and a plaster."

"Not a chance," I said. "Come on. We've got a curse to do."

Bill hopped up onto my arm and I stood up. I took my wand out and checked that it was working. I gave it a little shake and green sparks fizzed out, like they're supposed to. Then Bill and I marched up to the palace.

The guards on the door saw the look on my face and my fizzing wand. They didn't dare try to stop me.

But when I'd got past them, there was a snooty footman at the door asking for the golden invitations. He had a big pile of them on a small table. He asked me for mine. I laughed in his face, kicked the table over and stormed in.

They were all in there in the big hall. King, queen, baby, celebrities, courtiers, reporters, guests, you name it. The palace staff had pulled out all the stops. There were balloons and fancy nibbles and a great big pink and white cake. Above all their heads there was a huge banner that said:

WELCOME, PRINCESS BEAUTY

When I barged in, the Twelve Good Fairies were crowded round a frilly crib with their soppy gifts for the baby.

The baby was a nice little thing, actually. I could see that. She lay in her cradle and smiled and cooed at everyone. She didn't seem to mind being given Happiness and Wisdom and Health and whatnot, although I suspect she would have been just as happy with some mashed banana. Maybe I would magic some up for her later.

But first, I had a curse to deliver.

The Curse

Now, the curse.

I'm going to have to explain this carefully. A lot of people think I said something I didn't. They think I said, "*On her 16th birthday she will prick her finger on a spindle **and die**.*" But I didn't. I never said anything about dying. What I was *going* to say was, "*She will prick her finger on a spindle **and I** will give her a sticking plaster.*"

But I never got to say it. I had my wand out and

the thunder was thundering nicely. I got as far as,
"*On her 16th birthday she will prick her finger on a spindle **and I** ...*"

Say it out loud and you'll see the problem.

And then everyone started to scream and rush about, and I didn't get to say the last words. Which were pretty important. But it's hard to speak when the Captain of the Guard has got you in a headlock.

You're surprised to hear the truth, eh? I thought you would be. But you shouldn't believe those nasty rumours people like to spread about me. It's important to listen to both sides of a story.

I promise you, all I ever meant to do was to wait until the princess was older, then lure her into a quiet attic where no one would disturb us. Then she would prick her finger – nothing *too* bad, but there does have to be at least a tiny bit of nastiness or else a curse is not a curse.

But then I would give the princess a plaster to show her how nice and helpful I can be. We would have a long chat and I would tell her about how mean everyone was to me 16 years ago, when she was christened.

I would tell her about the Good Fairy club, and about how I didn't get invited to anything, ever. I would explain about the curse and how it was a protest at how unfair it all was, but how it was nothing personal and I never meant any real harm. The princess would see things from my point of view and she would be sure not to repeat the mistakes of her rude parents. We would become firm friends. She would invite me as guest of honour to her 16th birthday party.

But then everyone heard me wrong.

And, as a result, I was marched out by the Captain of the Guard, who still had me bent over in

a headlock. Bill dive-bombed him again and again from above, but the Captain of the Guard just batted him away. Bill didn't even get a peck in. He did his best, but he's not a pecker by nature. He lost quite a lot of feathers.

A Thousand Times Worse

Bill and I went home to nurse our wounds.

If the king and queen were going to be like that, I would let them think the worst. Think of all the trouble they were going to have for the next 16 years. They would have to ban spinning wheels all over the kingdom. It wouldn't make them very popular. They would probably ban pins and needles too, just to be on the safe side.

"Just wait until people's pants start falling down,"

I said to Bill. "When the elastic goes, there'll be no safety pins to keep them up. There'll be an outcry."

"I guess," said Bill.

"Wait until their clothes are all ragged and they can't make any new ones," I said. "The Good Fairies won't be able to buy any new dresses for their dances."

"Think of that," said Bill. "No shoppin' trips for clothes. What a world."

I think he was being sarcastic.

"OK, so it's not much of a revenge for what they did to me," I said, "but it's better than nothing."

"Hmm," said Bill.

"Anyway, it's only for 16 years," I said. "Then I can make it all right and get to move in royal circles again."

"That what you wanna do?" Bill asked.

"Well, I'd like to have the chance," I said. "Think

how jealous the Fairies will be when I'm best friends with the princess."

At that point, I hadn't realised that something unexpected had happened.

It was that silly little Fairy Violet who really messed things up. She got in on the act and made things a thousand times worse. After I'd been marched out the hall, she still had her gift to give, you see. She decided to be clever and soften the curse. The rules of magic let you have one go at doing that.

And so Fairy Violet changed my harmless "*and I*" bit to "*and fall asleep for a hundred years*". What a pest.

I know this because she came round and told me so. In fact, that night, all of the Fairies came round in an angry fluttering mob. I didn't invite them in, of course. They stood and shouted through the

letterbox. They wanted to tell me what a disgrace I was. I ignored them until they went away.

If only Violet hadn't meddled. Princess Beauty would have pricked her finger, we would have had our cosy little chat and the whole thing would have ended there. But, no. Violet thought she knew best.

There was nothing I could do about it. The curse was now well and truly cast, with Violet's bit of nonsense tagged on.

In 16 years, the princess could have had a plaster on her finger and me as a new best friend. But now the poor girl would be stuck with falling asleep for a hundred years. I had to go along with it. You can't mess about with the power of a curse.

Spinning Wheels and Broomsticks

You may wonder what happened over the next 16 years. Well, not a lot at first. I kept my head down. As you can imagine, I wasn't popular – what with all the trousers that were falling down and clothes that were falling apart at the seams since nobody was allowed to do any spinning or sewing or whatnot.

The Good Fairies were always coming round to throw eggs at my door. Bill enjoyed eating the eggs. The fairies' dresses were beginning to look quite shabby. I never went out to confront them. I just stayed in and only ever took my broomstick out at night, when there was no one around to shout "Boo!" at me.

It's boring, never going out. I found myself twiddling my thumbs with nothing to do. Bill made me buy a guitar, so I could play while he sang. It was funny, but I found I had a knack. I picked it up in no time. We spent some great musical evenings by the fire, me strumming away on the guitar while I learned Bill's songs. There were a lot of them. Most were about lonely flying and worm shortages.

I had a lot of time to think too. All right, so it wasn't my fault that Princess Beauty was doomed to fall asleep for a hundred years. But it wouldn't have happened if I hadn't messed about with curses in the first place.

Bill didn't say "I told you so", which was good of

him. I really should have listened to him. But it was too late now.

So there I was, 16 years later, up in the palace attic with my spinning wheel.

I pedalled away like an expert, although I can't say I was having fun. It was a wet night and I would rather have stayed at home. Balancing a spinning wheel on a broomstick in the rain is no joke. I had a wet crow huddled up against me too. But you have to show up when curses are involved. It's in the rules.

Bill was perched on a rafter, drying out and singing a song called "Slug Blues". It goes like this:

Woke up this mornin'
hopin' for some bugs,
early bird had got 'em
an' all that's left is slugs.

His warm, bass tones calmed me down a bit. I was glad to have him there. I was nervous. I needed my plans to go right.

Downstairs, everyone was busy getting ready for the birthday party. It hadn't started yet. The kitchen was in uproar. The king and queen were wrapping up presents in the throne room. Servants were blowing up balloons and polishing golden plates. No one had any time for the birthday girl.

So Beauty was bored and wandered up to the attic, just like she was supposed to do. It was the curse that made her, of course. "*She will prick her finger on a spindle.*" That's what I had said. I wish I hadn't. If I'd kept my big mouth shut, I could have been home by the fire with a cup of cocoa and my guitar.

"Hello," said Beauty, sticking her pretty head around the door. She didn't sound a bit scared – just curious. "Who are you, please?" she asked.

What a polite young woman, I thought.

"My name's Grimbleshanks, dear," I said. "Come on in." I did my best to smile like a harmless old lady.

"What are you doing, please?" she asked.

"Spinning," I said.

"Spinning," said Beauty. "Is that what you call it?"

"Why, yes," I said. "Haven't you ever seen a spinning wheel before, my dear?"

"No," she said. "Is spinning difficult? Can you show me how, please?"

"Oh no, my pretty one, it's not hard. It's easy. Do you want to try?"

Well, you know what happened next. I showed her how the spinning wheel worked, then she pricked her finger on the spindle, fell into a pile of wool and nodded off. Fast asleep she was, right there on the spot.

"That's it, then, Miz Grim," Bill said from his perch. "You done your bit."

"Yes," I said. "I have."

"Happy now?" said Bill.

I didn't say anything. I picked up a blanket I'd brought with me. I spread it over Beauty and tucked her in.

"Sorry, love," I whispered. "Not my doing." But she was fast asleep and didn't hear me.

Revenge isn't Sweet

The curse took effect straight away.

At the same time as Beauty pricked her finger, everyone else in the palace fell asleep. I didn't expect that. It wasn't in my curse or in the bit that busybody Violet added on either. But that's the trouble with curses. There can be unexpected side-effects.

Bill and I went down and had a look around. They were all frozen where they were.

The VILLAIN'S VERSION

The king and queen slept on their thrones in the great hall. In the kitchen, the cook was fast asleep with her hand raised to box the pot-boy's ears. I snapped my fingers under their noses and they didn't stir. It was spooky.

I stuck a pin in the Captain of the Guard – the one who'd had me in a headlock. Sadly, he didn't feel it.

"You can peck him if you like," I said to Bill.

"Nah," he said. "I ain't one for bearin' grudges."

We didn't hang about after that. Revenge wasn't sweet. Not at all. Beauty was a nice little thing. She didn't deserve this. Nobody did. Not even the Captain of the Guard.

I packed up the spinning wheel and we flew home. I had a strong cup of tea with four sugars, which usually makes me feel better. This time, it didn't.

Bill told me not to fret.

"What's done is done," he said. "It was a mistake, right? Don't beat yourself up."

I did, though. A hundred years is a long time to be asleep. Even if it wasn't my fault.

Well, not quite my fault. Like I said, it wouldn't have happened if I'd kept my temper in check and shown a bit more self-control.

Oh well. There was nothing to do now but wait it out.

In ten years, so many trees had grown up around the palace that you couldn't see it from the road.

I suppose I could have popped in and checked on what was happening inside, but I never felt like it. Anyway, I knew what was happening. The spiders would be spinning their webs and the dust would be gathering. There was nothing I could do about it. Why would I go there, just to stand around and crow? Crowing wouldn't help. Bill didn't want to crow either, and he *is* one – a crow, I mean.

Twenty years later, I'd got pretty good on guitar. Bill said I should buy a saxophone.

Thirty years later, I'd mastered the sax and

moved on to the clarinet. Life wasn't so bad. People were using pins and needles and spinning again. After all, the curse had happened, so there wasn't any point in keeping the ban going.

Forty years on, everyone seemed to have forgotten the whole business. People nodded to me in the Post Office and commented on the nice music they heard coming from my cottage.

Not the Twelve Good Fairies, mind. They hadn't forgotten. They always crossed the road when they saw me coming.

More years passed. Bill and I were asked to perform a little concert at the village hall. It went down rather well. We had a packed house.

The Fairies didn't come.

A Kiss, of All Things

So. A hundred years have gone by. A hundred years of Good Fairy dances, and I haven't been invited to any of them. Who cares? I don't need friends like them.

I've mellowed a lot. Well, a hundred years is a long time. We're all older and wiser now. I'm not so grumpy these days. I've made friends with a couple of local witches (Mrs Offal and Mrs Tripe) and a Wise Woman called Mrs Gumption. They wear black rags too.

I met Mrs Offal first, in the butcher's. She said she'd heard that I had a crow with a fine singing voice. She told me that she played the accordion.

"Really? You should bring it round one night," I said.

"I'd love to, Grimbleshanks," she said. "Tonight OK?"

That was a first! Me inviting a visitor round! I wasn't sure after I'd done it, but Bill said it was a great idea. We both cleared the place up, and I made some cakes and put a clean cloth on the table. I felt a bit nervous.

I needn't have. Mrs Offal came round and we had a fine old time. She said she had a friend who played the spoons (Mrs Tripe) and Mrs Tripe knew of a Wise Woman who played bassoon.

So now we've got a proper sort of group going. Bill sings, of course. We call ourselves the Big Bill

Beaky Band. We practise every Thursday. We drink a lot of tea. They bring sponge cake to share, and a selection of bugs for Bill.

Anyway. Tonight's the night. The curse will end, and I hope there will be a happy ending. I hope. But I'm not so sure.

Violet can never leave things alone. She just had to be the clever one who softened the curse, and then, would you believe, she added yet more stuff. A lot of extra details about a handsome prince who would wake Beauty with a kiss, of all things.

Nobody told me this to my face. I heard it from Mrs Tripe, who heard it from someone in the Post Office. For goodness' sake. I wish she'd stop dabbling. Violet, I mean. Why add a prince to make life difficult? Bill agrees. He thinks Beauty should enjoy herself before she settles down. He thinks 116 is way too young to get married.

I'm not a great fan of kissing either. Isn't it better to be woken by an alarm clock? Who'd want to be kissed before they'd brushed the cobwebs off and cleaned their teeth? A lot of dirt will have built up in a hundred years. It's a long time to go without a wash.

But maybe Beauty won't mind. After all, the prince will be handsome. That's a start.

Imagine sleeping for a hundred years. I bet she's ready for her breakfast.

Perhaps there will be another royal wedding before long.

They'd better invite me.

Or else.

The Big Bill Beaky Band

Bill Lead singer

Grimbleshanks Guitar, saxophone and clarinet

Mrs Offal Accordion

Mrs Tripe Spoons

Mrs Gumption Bassoon

BILL: *Ain't no good to lose your temper (strum, strum).*

Temper, temper (toot toot, wheeze).

No, it ain't no good to lose your temper (clink, clank, warble, strum).

If you aimin' for a happy life,

Oh yeaaaaaahh.

US: *Strum, toot, warble, clink, clank, wheeze, strum.*

The Wickedest WITCH in the World

ILLUSTRATED BY
Gerald Kelley

Well Done Me

HAH! Well done me!

I am the Wickedest Witch in the World!

Yes, it's official.

I've just won the "Wickedest Witch" contest!

I got a big silver cup with my name on the side.

Old Maggit
The Wickedest Witch in the World

That's what it said. I also got a black balloon, a baddy bag and a year's free supply of mint caterpillars from Yuckies, the sweet makers. Mind you, I've given Yuckies plenty of custom in the past. It takes a LOT of sweets to cover a whole house.

The other witches were a bit miffed. The Sea Witch turned green with envy – well, greener. Baba Yaga stormed out in a huff and wouldn't even stay for the party. She reckons she's famous back in Russia, or wherever she comes from. I say she's a bad loser, like the rest of them.

They all stood around giving me the evil eye and grumbling about the lack of comfy seats. We witches tend to be old. Chairs mean a lot to us. But not as much as giving little kiddies nightmares and winning contests.

The 13th Fairy took it worse than the others. She's called Grimbleshanks. She scuttled up to me at the supper table, where I was heaping my plate with yummy crispy spiders. The food is always good at these events. They know what witches like. As well as the plate, I was holding my winner's cup, a glass of fizzy wine, the black balloon and the baddy bag, so I had my hands full. It wasn't a good time, but I was up to it.

"Hello, Grimbleshanks," I said. "Well done on coming last."

"Shut up, Maggit," she said. "This is so unfair. You can't even spin. You never ride your broomstick. And I bet you've never ever put a whole palace of people to sleep for a hundred years."

"Hang on," I said. "I push little children into ovens. That's a lot more wicked than a daft little sleep spell."

She said, "Well, I think it's a scandal. I would like to remind you that you got pushed into the oven yourself in the end. By rights, you shouldn't even be here."

I said, "Ah, but I used a spell to put the fire out, didn't I? That took quick thinking. And look who's talking! This is the Wickedest *Witch* contest. You're not a witch, you're a fairy."

"A *bad* fairy," she snapped. "That's the same as a witch."

"Tell that to the judges," I said, with a sneer. "I won and you lost. Get over it." And I strolled off to have my picture taken.

The party didn't last long. Witches don't get on with each other at the best of times, never mind when they have just lost a contest. They all stayed just long enough to eat all the food, then the fighting began. There were the usual thunderbolts and flashes of green lightning and shouted curses. A number of people got turned into frogs and someone set fire to the curtains. It was quite a free-for-all.

I didn't join in. I had nothing to prove. I just stood there with a smug smile, drinking the fizzy wine and hugging my cup.

At last, everyone went home and I got the chance to inspect my baddy bag. There was a fake rubber worm, some cheap sparklers and a set of plastic fingernails. All around me, the staff were stacking up chairs, sweeping the filthy floor and chasing out the frogs. They made it very clear that I was in their way.

So I went home. I fed my cat, Wilson, and made myself a cup of tea. I set the silver cup in pride of place over the fire and sat down to look at it.

The Wickedest Witch in the World.

That was me.

It was a dream come true.

My Brilliant Idea

I suppose I should tell you how it came about. You'll have heard the story, of course. About the poor wood-cutter who took a new wife and let his dopey kids wander off into the forest. Hansel and Gretel, they're called. You're supposed to feel sorry for them, what with their rubbish parents and the way they get lost and have me to deal with and all. But there are two sides to every story.

I had been dying to win the Wickedest Witch title

for years, but I'd never even got on the shortlist. The contest is held every year and is always judged by the same three big cheeses. That's the White Witch from Narnia, the Snow Queen from somewhere up north and the Wicked Witch of the West. Her dressing room is full of crates of bananas because she always brings her troupe of flying monkeys. She's a bit of a diva, by all accounts.

Anyway.

Year after year, I filled out the form and sent it in. I had to write up to ten sentences to say why I felt I should be in the contest. Here's what I wrote:

My name is Old Maggit. I live in a house in the forest. I have a pointy hat and a cat called Wilson. I cackle over my cauldron (extra-loud at full moon). My favourite food is crispy spiders. My favourite colour is black. I am dead scary.

Every year, the contest people wrote back to tell me I had not been selected. They said that what I wrote could apply to pretty much any witch. There were some very wicked witches out there, they said, and I would need to do something much more dramatic if I wanted to stand a chance.

It had begun to get to me.

It was clear I needed to come up with something a bit different. Something that would make me stand out. Something so dark, so daring, so dreadful that it would pass into folklore as well as win me the cup. I thought about it all the time. I filled up a whole notepad with ideas, but they had all been done before or they weren't bad enough.

And then it came to me! An idea so brilliant that I couldn't believe nobody had thought of it.

I would make a gingerbread house and decorate it with sweets. A beautiful little house in the deep, dark forest that no kiddy could pass by. It would be the perfect honey trap.

At that point, I'll admit I hadn't really worked the whole thing out properly. Once the kiddies were in my power, I wasn't sure what I would *do* with them. But I felt sure I would come up with something. Perhaps I could hold them to ransom. Make them clean the cooker. Lock them in the naughty shed. At the least I would give them a stern lecture about not going into strangers' houses. Anyway, I would think about that bit later. I was keen to get started.

It made sense to do up my own house rather than build something new. After all, it only needed to be changed on the outside. That way, Wilson and I could carry on living there without any big changes. Wilson hates change. He likes his own cat flap, and his usual place by the fire.

I ordered the gingerbread panels for the walls

and the sweet decorations from Yuckies. They were quite surprised and kept asking if I was sure I needed so much stuff. It wasn't often they got such a huge order. As you might expect, it cost me a fortune, but I was sure that it would be worth it in the long run.

I got in a firm of local builders to do the real work. It's always best to use experts. It can get very messy when you're building with treacle and marzipan. And barley sugar windows are trickier than you would believe.

The builders were called Frank, Ted and Rocky. They did a lot of noisy hammering and caused no end of mess. I was glad when they finished. I was tired of them dragging icing

sugar into the house on their boots and demanding endless cups of tea.

The house took three days to complete. But, oh my! What a result! My humble cottage was gone. In its place stood a vision of chocolate roof-tiles, candy chimneys, marzipan windowsills, fudge shutters, lollipop flowers and toffee doors. I was so pleased, I even gave the builders a tip.

I said, "Here's a tip. Wipe your feet before you come into people's houses. Goodbye."

Well, I'm a witch. What do you expect?

The Kidnap

A sweet house has its downsides, to tell the truth.

Small forest animals and insects tend to get stuck to it. I was always going round peeling off rabbits and small hedgehogs and picking off flies.

The birds pecked off all the red Smarties, for some reason. But at least the sun didn't shine, so the roof didn't melt.

I felt sure that it wouldn't be long before some kiddies came along.

All I had to do was
sit inside, keep an eye on
the window and wait.

On the third day, I was in my chair by the window watching the sun set when I heard voices. Young high voices that rang through the forest. I ducked behind the curtain and crept across to the door.

My first victims! How exciting!

I stooped down and peered through the letterbox. Two children had appeared out of the trees – a boy of about twelve, I thought, and a small girl who looked about six. I'm not good with children's ages. Or children, come to that. I prefer cats.

The boy wore a coat and leggings and a stupid hat with a feather. The girl wore a green cape. She trailed behind the boy, crying loud sobs. Oh dear. A weeper. That could get annoying.

"Come *on*, Gretel!" the boy shouted. He sounded really bossy. "Why are you always so *slow*!"

The girl lifted her little wet red face and roared,

"I'm *hungry*, I'm telling you! I don't want to walk any more!"

"Too bad. Keep up. You're such a baby."

"I *hate* you, Hansel. I'm telling *Daddy*!"

The boy was just about to answer back, when he spotted my house. His mouth fell open. The girl followed his gaze and her eyes opened wide. I moved away from the letterbox. I didn't want them to see me peering out. That might put them off.

"Sweets!" I heard the boy shout. "It's a house made of *sweets*!"

The girl gave a squeal of joy. There came the sound of running feet, and then they were at the door.

"Get back!" the boy shouted. "*I'm* having the marzipan!"

"Well, I'm having the lollipop flowers, then."

"No you're not! I'm having the red ones!"

"I'm telling *Daddy!*"

Now was my big moment. They were right
outside. But I needed them *inside*. The moment they
set foot inside the door, they would be in my power.
That's the way it works. But they had to do it of their
own free will. I would need as much charm as I could
muster. I would normally throw the door open with a
wild cackle, but today that would not do.

I snatched off my pointy hat and threw it in a corner. It hit my broomstick, which fell over and hit Wilson. He spat at me.

"Sssh," I hissed. "Be a good boy, Wilson, if you please."

I put my hand on the door knob and called out in a gentle, shaky sort of voice.

"Who is that nibbling at my house? Little children, is it? I do hope so. I so *love* little children."

There was a moment's shocked hush.

I put on my best welcoming smile. Then I opened the door.

The boy stood staring at me. He had a chunk of gingerbread in one hand and a bunch of red lollipop flowers in the other. The girl had broken off the door knob and was getting stuck in. Her cheeks were all shiny and sticky. Some sugar was in her hair.

"Who are you?" the boy demanded. Talk about rude. I had to fight the urge to snatch off his daft hat and throw it in a tree.

"I'm the kind old lady who lives here," I said. "You can call me Old Maggit. And who might you be, deary?"

"I'm Hansel," he said, "and that's my sister, Gretel. If you *must* know."

"And what are you doing here, so far from the path?" I asked. "Are you lost?"

"No," said Hansel. "I'm running away from home. *She* just tagged along after me."

"He's always doing that," said Gretel as she broke off a piece of window-frame and stuffed it down her throat. "Running away, I mean."

"Any particular reason you run away so often?" I asked.

"I'm not happy with the food at home," said Hansel. He folded his arms and looked pompous. "I want to go to boarding school, where they have decent meals. But my stepmother says she and my father can't afford it. So I'm running away in protest. Can all of this house be eaten or just the outside?"

"Why don't you step inside and see for yourself?" I offered. "I'll make you a lovely mug of hot milk and some fresh bread and butter."

"Not likely," said Hansel. "We'll stick with the sweets."

"What about pancakes?" I said. "I'll let you toss them in the frying pan." That tempted them.

"*I* want to toss first," said Gretel, and made for the door.

"No," said Hansel. "*I* do. I'm the oldest." And he shoved her aside and pushed past me.

Gretel let out a scream and said, "I *hate* you, Hansel. I'm telling *Daddy*."

They really were most unpleasant children.

Into the Naughty Shed

Once they were inside, things didn't get any better. The two of them never stopped squabbling. I got out the eggs and the milk to make pancake batter. Gretel snatched the jug and spilt milk all over the floor. Then she walked in it. Hansel stepped on Wilson's tail and didn't say sorry. They were still too busy fighting about who would be first to toss the pancakes. Gretel kicked Hansel in the shin, and he got back at her by breaking an egg on her head.

She cried and pinched him on the arm. He pulled her hair.

"Look," I snapped. "If you two don't behave yourselves, there won't be any pancakes."

Gretel folded her arms, pouted and went into a sulk.

"In that case, I won't be staying," said Hansel, and marched to the door. He struggled with the knob, then said, "It won't open. What's going on?"

"I used a locking spell," I told him. "You're my prisoners now. If you look in that corner, you'll see a tall pointy hat and a broomstick. What does that tell you?"

"You're a witch!" cried Gretel, and burst into tears again.

Wilson fled upstairs, where it was quiet.

"Nonsense," said Hansel. "Open this door, vile old woman, or it will be the worst for you."

Now, I don't like being threatened, especially by hoity-toity children. I'm a witch. I deserve respect.

"Less of your back chat, young man," I snapped. "You're not at home now, you know."

"Wait till my parents hear about this," he said. "You'll be in trouble."

"Not as much trouble as you're in now," I told him.

Do you know what he did then? He started to kick the door. BANG! BANG! BANG! Between that and Gretel crying, I thought I'd go mad.

I grabbed him by the collar and put my face close to his.

"Hansel," I said. "I am giving you a warning. If you don't stop this now, I will lock you in the naughty shed. I mean it, mind."

He pulled away and attempted another run at the door. I almost caught him, but Gretel grabbed my apron string to hold me back, so the tip of his boot connected. BANG! The wood splintered. Flakes of paint showered down.

That did it. I was wild.

Ten minutes later, Hansel was locked in the shed. There's a little grate set in the door, and his angry red face pressed up against it as I walked away.

"Let me out!" he screamed. "Let me out, you wicked old witch!"

I went back into the house, where Gretel was throwing a tantrum. She lay face down, hammered the floor with her fists and howled.

"Get up," I said, my voice brisk. "Wash your face and hair in the sink. You're covered in egg and chocolate. Hands too. We need clean hands for cooking."

"We're cooking?" said Gretel. She stopped howling and sat up.

"Indeed," I said. "I said we'd make pancakes, and that's what we'll do. I'll teach you how to make good ones."

And I did. She was a bit slow and clumsy, but she seemed to enjoy herself. She told me that they never cooked at home. She said that they lived on takeaways because both her parents went out to work. Nothing wrong with parents working, of course. But I got the feeling that Hansel and Gretel were thrown into each other's company a lot. And their parents didn't seem to check them much. They had plenty of toys, she told me, but not a lot of time with their mum and dad. They ran away all the time just for something to do.

The pancakes turned out fine. We ate them with sugar and lemon. Gretel washed up. She was yawning and looking a bit tired, but she wanted to do it herself.

I took a plate of pancakes out to Hansel, who started up with his nonsense again the moment he saw me.

"Brute!" he shouted. "Kidnapper!"

I said, "Do you want these pancakes, or shall I take them away?"

He said, "Do they have sugar on?"

I said, "They do. And lemon."

He said, "Do you have any chocolate spread?"

I said, "No." If there's one thing I can't stand, it's a faddy eater.

He said, "All right. I'll have them I suppose."

I said, "What's the magic word?"

He said, "All right. Please."

I passed them through the grate and walked away.

He rattled the bars, kicked at the door and shouted, "How long do I have to stay in here?"

I said, "Until you stop kicking other people's property. You have to learn that bad behaviour has consequences. Goodnight." And I went back indoors.

Gretel and Wilson were playing with a piece of string.

She said, "Is Hansel all right? Did he like the pancakes?" She sounded all sweet and hopeful.

I said, "Yes. He loved them." And she beamed from ear to ear. When she's not crying, she's really not that bad.

She said, "He's not always like that. Only when he gets too tired."

I said, "Indeed. He needs a good night's sleep. We all do."

I made up a bed in the spare room. We each had a glass of warm milk. I read Gretel a story about evil fairies, which she enjoyed. Wilson sat on her lap and followed her upstairs when she went to bed.

I checked on Hansel before I turned in. I wasn't worried about him getting cold. There are plenty of old sacks in the shed.

I listened at the shed door. From the floor, there came the sound of heavy snoring. He was all right, then. He would be a lot less uppity in the morning, after a good night's sleep. I know how *I* feel when I stay up until all hours.

I looked in on Gretel. She was fast asleep too. Wilson was curled up on the bottom of the bed.

Result!

What Next?

The next morning, Gretel and I had porridge for breakfast, with cream and sugar. She looked much better now her face and hair were clean.

She had two bowls of porridge. We followed that with toast and honey. Then we cleared away the plates together. She washed and I dried. Then I showed her how to lay the fire. I let her light it with the matches. She loved that.

I left her showing Wilson the pictures in the

evil fairy book and went to check on Hansel.

His face was already at the grate. He wasn't so red now. He looked pale and a bit worried.

I said, "Morning. Sleep well?"

He said, "When do I get out?"

I said, "We'll see. What do you want for breakfast?"

He said, "What is there?"

I said, "Healthy porridge."

He said, "Is that all?"

I said, "Yes. Take it or leave it, up to you."

He said, "All right. I suppose so. I mean – um – yes, please."

Hey! We were getting somewhere!

I took him out a bowl of porridge and passed it through the bars. He grabbed at it. I held on.

I said, "What do we say?"

He mumbled, "Thank you."

His manners were a lot better already. I would let him out if he kept it up.

To my surprise, Gretel offered to go around the house peeling off flies. I was pleased about that, as it's not a job I enjoy. While she was gone, I drew up a chart on a big sheet of paper, which I pinned to the wall. I listed all the jobs that needed doing around the house, together with Hansel and Gretel's names. Each time they finished a task, they would get a gold star. If they got ten stars, they would get a treat. Good idea, eh?

Gretel came in with a basket of dead flies and got a star right away. I explained the chart system to her, and she was thrilled. I left her combing Wilson's tail and went to the woodshed.

"May I come out now, please?" asked Hansel in a very polite manner. "I'm very sorry."

"Of course," I said. I unlocked the door, and he

stepped out, looking nervous. I pushed his hat down over his eyes for a joke, and he smiled a bit. I took his hand. "Come on. Cheer up. Let's go in the house and I'll show you this lovely chart I've made."

Like Gretel, he was quite taken with the chart. Both of them stood quietly while I told them again how it worked.

"Right," Hansel said. "I'll go and chop some wood, then. That's a man's job."

Gretel opened her mouth to argue, caught my eye and shut it again.

"Gretel," I said. "I wonder if you would be so kind as to fetch in a bucket of water from the pump? The kettle needs filling. I'm gasping for a cup of tea."

"Of course, Old Maggit," she said, and ran off.

I sat down with the newspaper and Wilson on my

lap and left them to get on with the chores. It was wonderful.

We had home-made soup, bread, cheese and apples for lunch. We sat nicely at the table and had a very pleasant conversation. We passed each other things and said "please" and "thank you". They told me about their favourite colours and what they wanted for their birthdays. I told them about the Wickedest Witch contest. They were very interested. I told them all about the entry form and the many years of no luck. I told them a bit about the witches who got through most years. Those were the ones who sneered at me for not even making the shortlist.

"So you have to do something really, *really* wicked?" asked Gretel, with wide eyes.

"Yep," I said. "The sweet house was just for starters. Now I have to decide what happens next. With you two, I mean. It's a bit of a problem."

"You could send a ransom note," said Hansel. "Our parents will pay up. But I think they might be on holiday. They might not get it for weeks."

I hadn't thought of that.

"You could sell us as slaves," said Gretel. "To a pirate captain. You'd like that, wouldn't you, Hansel?" She turned to me and whispered, "He's always wanted to run away to sea."

"I don't know any pirates," I said. "Sorry."

"You could eat us," was Hansel's next idea. "Only joking," he added.

Gretel and I laughed.

I said, "Not likely. That daft feather on your hat might get stuck in my throat. Anyway, all that cheese has quite filled me up."

"Well," said Gretel. "You go and put your feet up, Old Maggit. We'll have a think about it, won't we, Hansel? While we finish the chores."

This was working out even better than I had imagined. Not only were they doing all my work, they were also doing my *thinking* for me.

"Another gold star each!" I cried, and sat down with the crossword puzzle.

The Plan

By supper time, the house was as clean as a new pin. There was a pile of logs by the back door, loose sweets had been swept up, the garden was free of weeds, the chimney had been swept and Wilson had been brushed to within an inch of his life.

Hansel and Gretel had earned nine stars each. Even better, they hadn't squabbled while they were doing it. They even helped each other out. Gretel sang as she worked. She had a terrible voice, but it was nice to see her happy. Hansel gave her kind little pats on the head whenever he went by. It was quite heart-warming.

We had baked potatoes for supper. I had a feeling crispy spiders wouldn't appeal to children.

"Old Maggit," said Hansel as he cleared the plates away (without being asked). "We've been thinking about your problem."

"You have?" I said.

"Yes. We think we've come up with the answer."

"Really?"

"Yes. We think you should tell a big fat lie on the entry form."

"You do?"

"Yes. We think you should say that you locked me in the woodshed and fattened me up."

"And made me be your slave," added Gretel, excited.

"And then say that you heated up the oven ready to cook and eat me," shouted Hansel.

"We know you wouldn't, of course," said Gretel. "Not really. It's only a story."

"So what do you think?" asked Hansel.

"I like it," I said. "It's got drama. It's got horror. It's got cannibalism. I'm pretty sure it's a winner. There's only one thing wrong with it."

"What's that?" they chorused.

"Well – that would be the end of you two, wouldn't it?" I said. "You'd never be able to show your faces again. Not if you'd been cooked and eaten. The second anyone saw you alive and kicking, it would all come out. I wouldn't be the Wickedest Witch in the World. I'd be a laughing stock."

They both thought about this.

"You could say we tricked you in the end," said Hansel. "We could make up a story where – I don't know – something like, Gretel could act stupid and say she didn't know whether the stove was hot yet, and you could look in, and she could push you inside."

"Pushed inside my own oven?" I said. "Hmm. Wouldn't work. You see, that would mean *I'd* be a goner. I'd have trouble filling forms in if I was burnt to a crisp."

"You could say you used a spell to put the fire out," said Gretel. "Then it would be a happy ending for all of us." For a six-year-old, she came up with some good ideas.

"And even if you don't kill us in the end, the wicked *plan* was there," said Hansel. "That's what's important."

"You know, you could be right," I said. "It might

just work. As long as the pair of you promise never to breathe a word of it to anyone."

"Of course we won't!" said Gretel, shocked. "It will be our secret."

"I'll help you fill in the entry form, if you like," offered Hansel. "I've got very neat writing."

"Excellent!" I cried. "Another gold star for each of you! That means you get a treat. What would you like?"

They opted for a go on my broomstick. Fair enough. We all squeezed on and had a nice little ride over the forest by the light of the moon. They giggled and screamed and we did a loop the loop, which I haven't tried in years. Hansel lost his hat. Gretel shouted, "Again! Do it again!"

It was a right laugh. A bit chilly, though.

How it Ended

They went home the next day. Hansel promised to post my entry form when they passed a post box. I offered them a basket full of sweets off the house, but they said no, thank you. I couldn't blame them. It was a warm day and the chocolate tiles were beginning to melt. Brown streaks oozed down the walls. Squirrels had been at the marzipan. The birds had picked off *all* the Smarties, not just the red ones. The house was definitely past its best.

"We'd like a slice of your home-made bread and a flask of soup, though," said Hansel. "If it's not too much trouble."

"Of course," I said. "It will be a pleasure." Well, I do make good soup.

Gretel gave me a big hug and said she wished I was her nan. Hansel showed me how to do something called a "high five".

Gretel asked if she could come and visit Wilson. I told her she could, but it had to be a secret. Hansel wanted to come and chop more logs in a couple of days. I told them both to leave it until I had a reply from the people at the Wickedest Witch contest. I didn't want to get put out at the last minute. You're not supposed to get visits from your victims.

We parted at the garden gate. They ran off hand-in-hand. I stood there waving long after they vanished into the trees.

Then I went in and took down the chart, put
away the jar of gold stars and made myself a cup of
tea.

I have to say, Wilson and I felt a bit lonely.

The next day, Frank, Ted and Rocky came to strip
all the soggy gingerbread and the last mucky sweets

off the house. Once that was done, there was nothing left to do. Everything went back to normal. No one called. I would have been glad of some company.

I cheered up when the postman arrived a week or so later with my invite to enter the contest. At long last, I was a contender! The big cheeses had believed the story we had concocted! They sounded rather impressed. I was in with an excellent chance.

Well, you know what happened. I showed up, and I won!

So. Here I am, gazing at my silver cup and wondering what to do with a rubber worm, some sparklers and set of plastic fingernails. Wilson's popped the balloon already.

Hang on! What's that? I think I heard the gate squeak! Could it be ...?

"Old Maggit!" comes Gretel's voice. "It's us! Did you win? Oh, do say you won!"

"Ready for some more logs?" shouts Hansel. "I've brought a better axe!"

Wilson leaps off my lap with a happy mew and runs to the door.

Yes. I'm the Wickedest Witch in the World – but children love me.

How weird is that?

Have Some WICKED FUN
with the Villains ...

Which Villain are You?
A Quiz!

Old Maggit's Wickedest Pancakes
A Recipe!

Which Villain are You?

Could you be the next Wickedest Witch in
the World? Or maybe you're more of a bad fairy ...
Take this quiz to find out which villain you are.

1. **You've received an invitation to the royal ball. The whole kingdom will be there, dressed up in their finest garb. What will you wear?**

   A. Black, black and more black. And you can't
   forget your signature pointy hat!

   B. Something comfy and practical – definitely no
   silly high heels.

   C. You'll go on a shopping extravaganza to find a
   stylish new dress. You're going to be the most
   dazzling guest of them all!

   D. An outfit in your favourite colour, with lots of
   ribbons and bows – perfect to catch the prince's
   eye.

   E. A wonderful colourful dress with a matching
   handbag, shoes and tiara.

2. When the big night arrives, how will you get to the palace?

A. On your broomstick, with your pet crow to keep you company.

B. You're starting to feel a bit too old for a broomstick – it would be much warmer inside a taxi ...

C. You'll have a driver waiting to pick you up in a sleek, shiny limo.

D. In a coach with a high roof, so that tall, elegant people like you won't bang their heads on it!

E. A horse-drawn carriage is the only way you plan to travel.

3. **You've finally reached the palace and it's time to enjoy the party. Where will you spend most of your time?**

A. You'll watch the band and enjoy the music – maybe you can ask them for some tips to improve your own skills.

B. You're going to find the comfiest seat in the room and stay there all night.

C. You'll be wherever all the other fashionable people are, of course.

D. You'll be in the ballroom, ready and waiting for the prince when he asks you to dance.

E. You'll be at the dinner buffet – maybe you can sneak a few cakes into your bag to take home.

4. **Not everyone is thrilled to see so many villains at the ball, and a rather unpleasant guest tells you that you shouldn't be there at all. How do you respond?**

A. You start thinking up a clever curse to teach them a lesson.

B. You give them a good telling-off for being so rude.

C. You ignore them for now, but when you get home you'll go to your secret lair and plot your revenge.

D. You tell them that they shouldn't dare say such a thing to the prince's future bride.

E. You show off your invitation to prove them wrong, and get back to enjoying the buffet.

5. After a long night, you've made it home. What are your plans for tomorrow?

A. You're meeting up with your friends for band practice.

B. You'll be sitting by the fire while you plan your entry for the next Wickedest Witch contest.

C. After you get back from the shops, you'll keep an eye on your enemies in the Seeing Pool.

D. You're going to wind up the servants by playing pranks on them.

E. You're planning to have a long lie-in while you wait for the butler to bring you breakfast in bed.

Now turn over to find out which villain you are ...

ANSWERS

Mostly **A**s
You're Grimbleshanks

Mostly **B**s
You're Old Maggit

Mostly **C**s
You're the Queen

Mostly **D**s
You're Angula

Mostly **E**s
You're Lardine

Old Maggit's Wickedest Pancakes

"I said we'd make pancakes, and that's what we'll do. I'll teach you how to make good ones."

Here's a recipe for some delicious pancakes like the ones Old Maggit teaches Gretel to make ...

Ingredients

- 150g plain flour
- ½ teaspoon salt
- 1 tablespoon baking powder
- 1 teaspoon caster sugar

- 225ml milk
- 1 egg
- 1 tablespoon butter, melted
- 150g blueberries

Method

1. Measure the flour, salt, baking powder and caster sugar into a bowl and mix well.

2. Add the milk, egg and melted butter, then beat everything together until the mixture is smooth.

3. Add the blueberries and mix.

4. Heat up a frying pan and lightly grease it with butter.

5. Pour a large spoonful of batter into the pan and leave it to cook until bubbles appear on the surface of the pancake.

6. Flip the pancake and cook for a couple of minutes on the other side.

7. Repeat until you've used up all the pancake batter.

8. Serve with whatever toppings you like best! Will you choose sugar and lemon like Old Maggit, or do you prefer Hansel's favourite – chocolate spread?

The Weirds have moved into No. 17 Tidy Street, and Pinchton Primm's quiet life will never be the same again ...

Kaye Umansky

Just Plain WEiRD

Beware of Normal!

illustrated by Chris Mould

978-1-78112-791-9